THE WALL: BOOK TEN OF BEYOND THESE WALLS

A POST-APOCALYPTIC SURVIVAL THRILLER

MICHAEL ROBERTSON

EDITED AND COVER BY ...

To contact Michael, please email:
subscribers@michaelrobertson.co.uk

Edited by:

Pauline Nolet - http://www.paulinenolet.com

Cover design by Dusty Crosley - https://www.deviantart.com/dustycrosley

COPYRIGHT

The Wall: Book ten of Beyond These Walls

Michael Robertson
© Michael Robertson 2021

The Wall: Book ten of Beyond These Walls is a work of fiction. The characters, incidents, situations, and all dialogue are entirely a product of the author's imagination, or are used fictitiously and are not in any way representative of real people, places, or things.

Any resemblance to persons living or dead is entirely coincidental.

All rights reserved.

No part of this publication may be reproduced, stored in a retrieval system, or transmitted in any form or by any means electronic, mechanical, photocopying, recording, or otherwise, without the prior written permission of the author except in the case of brief quotations embodied in critical articles and reviews.

CHAPTER 1

Artan stood amongst his crew. Matilda on his left. Nick on his right.

Olga tutted. "Another wall?"

While only about twenty feet tall, the wall before them loomed large enough to pose a challenge. Another barrier they would struggle to scale. Like many other structures since they'd passed through the funnel, it had been built from steel. Artan stepped forwards, the ground soft beneath his feet. He pulled the small bush aside with his left hand and pointed at the tunnel with his right. "Except we don't have to climb this one."

"Well, what are you waiting for, then?" Olga said.

Artan stepped back as if shoved by her response. Every word Olga had delivered since Max's death came charged with aggression. Every response an open challenge to anyone who wanted it.

"What's that face for?" she said.

Artan let the bush fall back across the tunnel. He stepped towards his friends, letting the silence hang long enough to show Olga he had no interest in a row. "It's not dark enough yet. We need to come back later. Can you take us to the safe house, Gracie?"

Grace looked at Artan with a glassy stare while she rubbed her chest with her right hand.

"Gracie?"

"Huh?"

"The safe house? Can you take us there?"

Paler than usual. And why wouldn't she be? She'd lost the only family she'd had. And while Aus might have been a weapons-grade arsehole, she'd still lost her brother. Taken his life, in fact. Artan shuddered. Seeing Gracie in this state took him back to his cell in Edin. The time he'd spent alone when he had nothing else to do but accept he'd taken another person's life. The life of someone he loved. No matter how evil, no matter what the bastard had done, he'd still killed his dad. "So?"

"Yeah," Gracie said. "Safe house. Right. Come on, let's go."

The walled community at their back, Artan walked beside Nick, hugging himself to protect against the chill of the impending night. The wind blew hard across the open meadow. Maybe he should be more like the long grass around them. Maybe he should accept the greater power of nature. Relax and go with it. Instead, he pulled his shoulders to his neck and gritted his teeth. Pains ran from the bottom of his jaw to his ears.

"So what's the plan?" Olga said, hooking a finger into her collar and loosening it. "How is entering that place going to help us get over the wall?"

"None of the doors in that place have handles," Nick said.

Olga's eyes bulged. "This is going somewhere, right?"

"Instead," Nick said, "they have removable magnetic handles."

"So they do have handles?"

"To get into any of the buildings," Nick said, raising his voice, "you have to have a handle to open the doors."

"That doesn't sound very secure, and I still don't know why you're telling us this."

The others, including Artan, kept their lips pressed tight. The already hostile Olga had turned it up to eleven, but Nick didn't know her as well as the others, so he approached her with less caution. "It's secure if you keep the handles hidden. It made it hard for us to rob them whenever we went in. We had no idea how the doors opened until Artan worked it out."

Artan held his breath in the face of Olga's scrutiny. "How did you do that?" she said.

Although Artan opened his mouth, Nick cut him off. "He climbed into a building and barged the door open from the inside. It was still an inelegant way to rob them, but an open door was much better than anything we'd managed until that point."

Olga threw her arms in the air. "And what's this got to do with the magnetic handles?"

"Were it not for Artan falling into the dog pit—"

"You make it sound like I was being clumsy." Artan stumbled on a molehill. The fading light made it harder to pick a safe path.

Nick smirked behind tightened lips. A glint flared and died in his eyes. "Anyway," he said, "regardless of how we found the handles, what I'm getting at is Artan fell into a pit filled with dogs. I went down there—"

"As you should have. You were the reason I fell."

"And I take my share of the credit. We fought the dogs back together, and when we left the pit, Artan found a handle that opened all the doors. It gave us access to every building in the place. Including their armoury. That was how we got so many weapons into Dout."

"For what good it did." Olga snorted. "That was hardly a resounding success, now, was it?"

Gracie slumped but kept her attention straight ahead, her loose strands of hair whipping in the wind. Artan rested a hand on her back.

"You're missing the point, Olga," Nick said.

"Or maybe you're shit at making one?"

Nick laughed.

Olga stopped walking. She stood with a widened stance and balled fists.

Nick slipped his bag from his shoulder, plunged his hand inside, and removed the handle Artan had given to him when he'd nearly left Dout. A round magnetic plate. The handle had a bar about an inch thick and eight inches long. He offered it to Olga.

The tension left her when she took it and turned it over in her hands. They'd gone far enough from the community they intended to rob for the main wall to dominate the horizon once again. "And how will this little thing help us get over that wall?"

"If we can get more of those magnets, we can tie them together and use them to climb the wall. Magnets like metal."

"You think I don't know that?"

"The wall's metal."

"Again, stating the obvious."

William held his hand up to Olga. Her already red face turned a deeper shade of crimson. But he focused on Nick. "Do you think we can get enough magnets? I like the idea, but how many will it take?"

"We'll get enough," Artan said. "There must be thousands of them in there."

"Yet you've only found your first one recently?" Olga said. "How many times had Aus and his crew of incompetents been inside that place previously? And what if you go in there and get caught? We should come with you."

"As you rightly say, Olga," Nick said, "we've been robbing them for years. While we've only just found the handles, we have plenty of experience in searching the place for supplies. Both this community and the one we take the solar panels from are very quiet at night. We can get in and out without being seen or heard."

"It won't help to have more of us with you?" William said.

"No." Artan shook his head. "We'll be better on our own. We'll be quieter. We know the place well enough to move quickly through it." Before anyone could comment, he said, "How much farther is this safe house, Gracie?"

Gracie pointed at a dark forest in the distance. Artan's stomach tensed when she replied in monotone, "It's in there."

THE CONVERSATION DIED as they closed in on the forest. At least it put a cork in Olga. William, Matilda, and Olga all held swords. Artan and the others had spears, and they carried spares in sheaths on their back. They also had knives at their hips. A spear rarely flew true with so many obstacles in the way.

"Are you sure this is a good idea?" Olga said.

Gracie continued walking and entered the forest.

Pushing on with leaden steps, Artan followed her. A rich tang of soil hung in the air. The thick canopy reduced his visibility to about ten feet.

The others followed. The crunch of leaves and snapping twigs played a symphony of their progress. Hard to keep the noise down in a place like this. It seemed all the louder for the reduction in visibility. But it worked both ways. Every hair on Artan's body stood on end. He listened for the enemy with every atom of his being.

Using the tip of his spear to feel the way, Artan held it out ahead of him. He tapped trees and branches so he didn't walk into them.

Olga now at the back, she said, "What the fuck is this place, Gracie?"

The rustling of creatures scuttled away from them.

"This is like some kind of screwed-up fairy tale," Olga said.

Gracie paused and stepped aside to let Artan and the others past. She waited for Olga to catch up. "First, shouting at me isn't helping anyone. Second, we need somewhere secluded. This is that place." An owl hooted in the trees. "Unless you have anything better to offer?"

What little light made it through the forest's thick canopy caught the tightening and clenching of Olga's jaw. Her flared nostrils. Artan tensed and leaned forward, resting his weight on his toes. But Olga relaxed and stepped back. She dropped her attention to the ground.

Breathing through her nose, her chest rising and falling, Gracie relaxed. She nodded, reached across, and put a hand on Olga's shoulder. "I'm truly sorry for your loss."

Olga's head snapped up, and she fixed on Gracie. Her tense features cracked. A glaze spread across her wide glare. The rage that had thickened her words thinned. "And I yours."

Gracie nodded again and moved on. Passing the others, she stared straight ahead and led them away.

The darkness hid the cottage like it had everything else in the forest. Nothing one moment, and then an old rickety one-storey building just a few feet away. It had a wonky red-tiled roof. It had been constructed from large grey stones of differing shapes and sizes. The windows and door frame were all canted. The off-kilter construction belonged to a different time. A time that cared little for right angles. But, apparently, they cared about building houses that were made to last.

The cottage had a steel door fashioned to fit the leaning door frame. One of the few renovations to this ancient building. It hung slightly ajar. Gracie pushed it open, retrieved a torch from her bag, and turned it on. She'd been right to keep her light a secret. One of them would have insisted she used it sooner.

A mixture of damp and dust thickened the air and plugged Artan's nostrils. He shivered. The bare stone made it colder inside the cottage than out. They'd entered what had to be the main room. A space large enough to accommodate all of them. It had a fireplace that taunted them. Dared them to use it. Dared them to reveal their position with a trail of smoke. A small hallway led from the main room. It had a doorway on either side. Each led to a smaller room.

Gracie closed the door, and Olga said, "I still say you should let us come with you."

Nick reached across and rested a hand on Olga's forearm. "Please trust us when we say we need to do this on our own."

For all her front, Olga had quietened since her moment with Gracie. Her voice caught in her throat, her words strangled when she said, "But how will we know if there's a problem? What if you need our help? We've already los—" Her face turned puce. She coughed into her clenched right fist.

The same bag she'd pulled her torch from, Gracie removed two walkie-talkies. She handed one to Olga and one to Artan. "I managed to get these two before Freddie took the rest. They have the range. If Artan uses his, you'll hear him and be able to help."

"You'll call if you need us?" Olga said.

Artan nodded. "Yeah. But please don't worry. We'll be fine."

Olga threw her arms around Artan. Pulling him down to her height, she squeezed. "You'd best be."

Other than the magnet inside Nick's, both Artan and Nick had empty bags slung over their shoulders. "I think by the time we get back to the community, it'll be dark enough to go in," Artan said. "You ready to leave?"

"Yeah." Nick opened the door.

"Let us know if you need us," Matilda said.

Artan nodded again and stepped outside. Nick stepped out beside him. He led Nick away, his steps crunching and popping beneath him. His stomach turned backflips as he picked a slow path back through the darkness. The cottage's door closed behind them. The *clunk* of a bolt slid into place. He gripped the walkie-talkie. Hopefully, he wouldn't need to use it. Hopefully, they'd be coming back in a few hours, their bags filled with magnets, and their plan ready to put into action.

CHAPTER 2

Gracie ruffled and twitched her nose, but it did little to prevent the damp atmosphere from snaking up her nostrils. Every time she moved around the abandoned building, pacing back and forth across the sandy floor, dust motes swirled in the air, floating through the torch's powerful beam. She scanned the room, the shadows shifting and changing in response to the inquisitive torchlight.

The main room had just one small window with a deep ledge. Olga sat on it, slipped her hand into her sleeve, and turned her back on the rest of them to rub the dirty pane. For what good it did. The darkness outside so complete, the window might have been cleaner, but it remained a black mirror, shining Olga's enquiry back at her. Maybe it would help if Gracie turned off her torch.

As much as Gracie wanted to tell Olga that Artan and Nick were long lost to the shadows, she kept it to herself while her friend continued to stare out of the window, her knuckles white from where she gripped the walkie-talkie. Olga's voice echoed in the small bay window. "How long do you think they'll be?"

Gracie shivered, the cottage colder on the inside than out. She clenched her jaw against the chill as if biting down might somehow help. How could they guess how long it would take them? But with Olga wanting a row with every interaction, she kept her lips pressed as tight as her jaw.

"I've not been here for years," Gracie finally said. Her voice betrayed her, a weak warble undermining her words. "Dad used to bring me and Aus here about once every six months. He often made us lead the way." She filled her lungs with the damp and dusty air and swallowed against the combined itch and lump in her throat. "He wanted to know we could find the place on our own …" She exhaled hard.

Rubbing her eyes, Gracie said, "If there were ever any problems with Dout, this is where he wanted us to come."

Matilda slipped her hand into Gracie's. Despite their frigid environment, she had a warm touch.

"We used to make a weekend of it." Gracie's smile held the weight of her buckling face. "Dad made it super fun. We made a fire. We hunted. We treated it like a holiday, some time away from Dout. All the while, Dad prepared us so we'd be self-sufficient. Maybe he knew this day would come. Although, I'm sure he hadn't guessed it would be my fault."

"It wasn't!" Matilda squeezed Gracie's hand harder.

"We ate rabbits and pheasants," Gracie said, "and sometimes deer. Although deer are much easier to catch in the north on the other side of the ruined city. But we did all right. Enough to keep us going for as long as we needed to be here. I think Dad imagined that if we ever put his plan into action, it would be as a pair. Brother and sister surviving together. I did too." She shook her head. "As a kid, I only ever saw it as time away. A small holiday from Dout." Her cheeks now damp with her tears, she shrugged. "It took a few years for me to see the anxiety in people's faces at Dad leaving. I think they often assumed he wouldn't come back. Who would run Dout in his place?"

Matilda clung onto Gracie's hand. "I'm really sorry."

Gracie threw her shoulders up in a shrug. "We've all lost someone. We're all hurting. I don't mean to go on about it."

"And it's not like we can do anything about it." Olga twisted her fists into her thighs, and the tendons in her neck pulled taut. "We need to suck it up and move on." She returned her attention to her dark reflection. A thin sheet of glass separated her from a diseased that could be sprinting towards the cottage right now. She either didn't consider it or didn't care.

"We should cover that window," Gracie said.

"What?"

"Put a sheet up or something. One of our empty bags. That way, we can keep the torch on and remain hidden. Also, there's something I need to do. I've been thinking about it since we left Dout."

Olga stood up, retrieved one of the empty bags from the floor, and looped it over two rusty nails so it hung down in front of the window. "What are you talking about? You're not making much sense."

"No, sorry." Gracie let go of Matilda's hand and gave her the torch. "Take this. I'll be back soon."

"What? Where are you going?"

"I have to go back to Dout."

"Are you mad?" Olga's face flushed. A vein lifted on her temple. "What can you possibly want to get down there that's of any use?"

"You're right, what I need to get has no use or purpose; they're purely sentimental. I want to get Mum and Dad's wedding rings. They're in Dad's room."

"And they're worth dying for?" Olga said.

"I get what you're saying, and I appreciate your concern."

"It's more than concern. It's good sense. Dout's filled with diseased."

"They're contained down there. The doors are closed off."

"And what if more soldiers come back?"

"In the middle of the night? That's exactly why I have to go now. This is my chance. It's not like we're coming back here after we've crossed to the other side of the wall."

"And what if Artan and Nick need you?"

"They have you lot on standby."

Olga clung to the walkie-talkie like she might use it as a weapon. "But—"

"Does the reward justify the risk?" Matilda said.

Gracie nodded. "Yeah. It does. We're on a journey, right? Hoping we'll find something when we go south?"

"Right."

"But we don't know where we're heading or what we'll find."

Since leaving Dout, Hawk had pulled into himself and spoke infrequently. "What's your point?" he said. "Are you changing your mind about crossing the wall?"

"No, I'm just changing my mindset. I don't know about you lot, but very little in my life has turned out how I envisioned. I expected to have a mum and dad for a lot longer."

"I'm sure we all did," William said.

"I expected to remain in Dout. Maybe help run it in the future. I'm learning that we can plan all we like, but things rarely pan out. Uncertainty is a way of life. All we have in this world is our intention."

"And you intend to die?" Olga said.

Gracie laid her right palm against her chest. "We don't know where we're heading, and even if we knew exactly and had a watertight plan on how to get there, we still might never reach our destination. I'm okay with that, but I need to shift my focus to this moment. I can't compromise the now to serve an imagined future. The best choice for me is to find my mum and dad's wedding rings. They'll make me feel better. At this moment, that's about the only thing I'm sure of. I'm with you all. I will still plan and hope for a better future on the other side of the wall, but I won't chase it to the exclusion of the now. If I don't go looking for those rings, I will forever regret it. Call me sentimental, but I need to do this."

A slight unwinding of her frame, Olga lowered the walkie-talkie, and her voice softened. "You know what? If I'd adopted that attitude with Max, things would be different. We'd all still be alive. Dout wouldn't have fallen. Maybe survival is the best we can hope for in this world, and while we have it, we need to honour the moment more. What you're about to do is mad, but what about this life is sane?"

Gracie smiled. "Thank you, Olga." She let go of Matilda's hand and stroked her back before walking to the steel door. "I'll be as quick as I can."

The door as cold as everything else in the cottage, Gracie slid the bolt free. She pulled it wide, stepped out into the night, and closed it behind her. The darkness pressed in, and the forest seemed to hold its breath. Then an owl hooted. The same one? And did it mean something? Had it seen her future? Should she give up on the idea of the rings now? Were they worth dying for? What would her dad think? She faced the sky. There were small breaks in the dense canopy. They revealed thick grey cloud punctuated by clusters of stars. "I know I've gotten to the safety of the cottage like we planned, Dad, but I have to do this. You understand, right?"

Gracie jumped when the door opened behind her. William stepped out and closed it again. "I can't let you do this on your own. Were I in your situation, I'd be going back into Dout too. I often think about what I left behind in Edin. You have a chance to live without those regrets."

William stood close, and with him being a few inches taller than her, she angled her neck to take in his face. His features set. His eyes calm. The reassurance she needed beside her right now. Her voice weak, she said, "Thank you."

CHAPTER 3

"I feel useless!" Olga paced the cottage's main room. Seven steps from one side to the other. She reached the wall, turned around, and strode back across the sandy floor to the other end. She passed the bolted steel door. The window with the makeshift curtain.

Matilda and Hawk sat on the floor and tracked her movement, their exhaustion hanging from their slack expressions. Olga threw her arms up. "I should have gone with Gracie. I know William said he had it covered, but I should have gone too. What's the alternative? Wait here all night?"

Olga paused. Matilda and Hawk continued watching her. "Go on," she said.

"Go on what?" Matilda said.

"I can see you want to say something, so do it. Get it off your chest." She held her hands as fists at her sides and pulled her shoulders back.

Matilda, unflinching, maintained eye contact. "Gracie's better off without you right now."

"You would side with William, wouldn't you?"

"Only because he's made the right call. He's the best one

to be with Gracie. She needs someone with a level head beside her."

Heavy breaths rocked Olga's frame. Hawk dropped his attention to the floor, but Matilda continued to stare at her. "Are you saying I'm a liability?"

Matilda's eyes flicked to the door. "You need to quieten down."

"You need to fuck off."

"Take the opportunity for what it is, Olga. Rest. Get your head together. Take the time we're being given. We all need it."

"Me especially?" Olga said.

Matilda pointed at the door. "It won't be long before we're climbing that wall, and who knows when we'll next get the time to rest after that."

"Is that why you've stayed here? You need the rest?"

"I do need the rest, we all do, but I'm staying here for Artan. If he needs me, I want to make sure I'm available. Why wouldn't I take the time to recuperate while I'm waiting? Although, arguing with you certainly isn't the rest I was hoping for."

Olga dragged the room's damp air in through her nose. "You know what, Matilda? Fuck you."

"I'm just trying to help."

"By telling me to sit down and be quiet? I can express myself however I see fit."

"You can. And I'm only suggesting you take this time to look after yourself. Also, if I feel attacked, I'm going to defend myself."

"I'm not attacking you."

"Hawk?" Matilda said.

He winced at Olga like looking at her caused him pain. "I understand why you're angry."

"I'm angry because I'm not happy being sidelined. Is that

such a crime?"

"Look, Olga," Matilda said, "we're all upset. And not as much as you or Gracie. How could we be?"

Olga pointed at Matilda. "Don't you dare!" The lump in her throat turned her words into a strained wheeze. "Don't you fucking dare! This isn't about Max."

"It's not?"

"No!" Olga stamped her foot. Her right knee tingled from the shock, the hard stone beneath the layer of sand unforgiving. "It's about me having something to offer. We've just come from a community that sidelined women, and now it's happening all over again. How come you're not pissed off about being shoved into a shitty house in the middle of a fucking forest with nothing to do? I should have gone with them. I should be doing more. This is bull—"

Olga's stomach sank. A gentle tapping on the other side of the window. The swishing of the trees outside from where the wind shook the forest. The tapping from where a branch hit the pane. The empty bag hanging as a makeshift curtain shifted, a slight breeze coming through the old window. She'd heard that tapping before. Not wood against glass, but enamel. The tap of teeth and the snorting of a bunged-up nose like a truffling animal. Both Hawk and Matilda stared at the window. Their jaws hung loose.

"Don't!" Hawk said.

Olga halted mid-step. But ignoring it wouldn't make it go away.

"Olga," Hawk said again, "leave it."

The ticking continued. The tapping. Teeth against glass. Snorting breaths. Olga gripped the bag curtain in a shaking grip. One last glance at Hawk and Matilda, she tore the curtain away, and Matilda shone the torch on the window.

Wide red eyes. Unperturbed by the torch's bright glare. The creature shrieked.

CHAPTER 4

"Jeez!" Artan jumped back. A face had appeared in the window. He pressed his right palm to his hammering heart and shoved Nick back with his left. "My god, don't do that to me."

Nick smiled at his own reflection. "I thought it would be quite funny to pop up behind you." He shook his head. "No?"

"No." Artan smiled despite himself. They were deep in a residential part of the walled community. Small one- and two-storey steel buildings everywhere. The larger commercial buildings might have had the potential to provide a better yield of magnets, but the first few they encountered were in use. Whereas most of the lights in most of the houses were off. Many of the citizens were sleeping or out. "It's hard to know which houses have people in and which don't."

"Maybe we should assume they all do?" Nick said. He squinted up at the moon. "We've been lucky to find as many empty houses as we have so far. But it's late enough for most people to be asleep."

"What are you saying? We sh—get down!" Artan dragged Nick beneath the window they'd been peering through. A light had come on in another room. He leaned against the cold steel wall, and his bag filled with magnets attached to it. The fabric muted the connection, but now they'd attached, how easy would it be to pull them free?

Nick crouched beside Artan, his mouth hanging open from where he stared up at the illuminated pane directly above their heads.

A man inside the house pressed his nose to the glass, turning it into a snout. Condensation formed from his breaths. He cupped the sides of his face, but his glazed eyes suggested he'd seen nothing. Too bright in his room. Too dark outside.

The man pulled away, and the light above blinked out.

Nick spoke in a whisper. "We've been lucky until this point."

The bottom of Artan's trousers were soaked with dew. They lay cold against his skin. He pulled his right trouser leg away, only for the fabric to settle against his shin again. "So what do you suggest we do?"

"We have two choices." Nick held up two fingers on his right hand. "We either keep searching and hope we find more empty houses. Or we try the next one with the lights off and tread lightly. How many more magnets do we need?"

"Three between us," Artan said. "You sound like you've decided."

"Most of the magnets have been by the front doors. Unless you have a compelling argument for us to go deeper into this place? But, in my mind, the farther we go in, the longer it's going to take us to get back out again, and the harder it will be to escape if we get rumbled. We reckon there's ten thousand people living inside these walls. I don't fancy having to get through them on my way out of here. The ammo runs worked so well because we could get in and out close to their armoury. This is a whole different matter. And I'm not sure how we'll cope if they release the hounds."

"Okay, fine." Artan wrapped the handle from his bag around his hand and tugged. But the magnets remained attached to the building's steel exterior. He yanked again, bracing against the wall with his right foot. On his third attempt, Nick helped, and the bag came free. "Let's stash the magnets and go into one of these houses each."

Nick led them away at a crouched run, around the side of another two-storey home nearby. Like many of the houses in the place, it had several windows, the lights out in every room. Nick shoved his bag into a bush out the front, reached in, and pulled a magnet free.

Placing his bag close to Nick's, but not so close they clung to one another, Artan also liberated a magnet for himself.

"This house seems as good as any," Nick said. "You want this one, and I'll go next door? Then we meet back here?"

Artan shrugged. "Sure."

With every house they'd broken into, Artan's body had wound tighter. They'd been lucky so far, but it only took one mistake … Maybe they should have persevered with the communal buildings. Surely most of them would have been empty at this time of night. But wherever they went, they were risking capture. They just needed to get on with it. Get in. Get out. Get back to the others.

Thunk! The magnetic handle attached to the front door. His teeth clamped on his bottom lip, Artan tugged once, and it opened. He twisted the handle, the magnet gritty against the brushed steel. It came free. The walkie-talkie at his hip, the magnet in his right hand, he slipped into the house, leaving the door slightly ajar. If he got through this place, he didn't need to be announcing his exit by barging the door open on his way out.

The houses' interiors stood in stark contrast to the harsh

brushed steel on the outside. The walls shone with a transparent coating. Like a thick layer of varnish, it held the heat and took the edge off the rough metal. Comfy chairs, children's pictures, a bookshelf in one corner.

The back of the front door. The first place Artan checked for a handle. He'd been lucky to find them there several times already. An easy bounty. He took them, didn't push his luck, and moved on to the next. But there were none here.

A small hallway about eight feet long ran from the living room to the kitchen at the back of the house. The place dark, Artan's eyes itched as he scanned the shadows. He walked on tiptoes, his heartbeat the loudest thing in the house.

Artan passed a set of stairs on his left on his way to the kitchen. The moonlight shone in through the window at the far end. Bright enough to cast a dull highlight over everything. No handles in here.

Footsteps upstairs.

"Shit!" Artan backed against one of the kitchen walls.

A light flicked on, the glow finding its way down the stairs and through the kitchen doorway. It lay along the floor in a neatly widening beam.

The magnet for opening the door in his right grip, the walkie-talkie on one hip, his knife on the other. Artan raised the magnet, ready to punch whoever walked through that door. What a snake! He'd broken into someone's house and now had plans to assault them.

Bare feet against metal, the person padded down the stairs. Every step closer. Every beat of Artan's heart slamming through him.

The person stepped clear of the bottom step.

Artan fought to regulate his breathing.

But the person walked into the living room and turned on the light.

Hard to tell from the back, but the man appeared to be in

his late thirties. His hair was dishevelled from where he'd clearly been in bed. He had a circular bald patch on his crown a few inches in diameter. How long before he admitted defeat and shaved it all off? He walked with the heavy, plodding steps of someone straight from sleep. He pulled his front door closed.

Artan burst from his hiding spot and went for the stairs. Taking them two at a time, he ran up on tiptoes, reaching the top as the man headed back towards the kitchen.

Waiting on the landing, Artan stepped towards the stairs and froze. The man didn't head for the kitchen. "Shit!"

Two bedrooms on the first floor. The light on in one, the door wide open. Someone slept in the double bed. The door to the other room hung ajar by just a few inches. Artan slipped inside. He could get out of the window and vanish before the man found him.

The door squeaked when Artan returned it to its original position. During the day, the general hum of an active community would have buried the hinges' barely audible groan. But at this time of night, it whispered to the man climbing the stairs: There's someone in your house.

Like he'd done in the kitchen, Artan pressed his back to the wall, this time behind the door. If he needed to, he'd knock this man out. But he'd only blow their cover as a last resort. Better they were in and out of this place unseen.

Artan hadn't had time to check the bedroom before he entered. It had two single beds. Two small sleeping forms. Girls. Maybe twins, they were both tiny. They couldn't have been any older than six. What was he doing sneaking around in children's bedrooms? Had it really come to this?

The door to the room swung open, hiding Artan behind it. He held his breath and pushed his back into the wall. He unclipped his walkie-talkie. If he blew their cover, he needed to let the others know. He might need their help.

The light from the hallway filled the room. The man's steps went to one bed and then the other. The gentle smacking of lips from where he planted a kiss on each sleeping child.

The walkie-talkie trembled in Artan's grip.

The man left and pulled the door to again. Artan sank and stumbled away from the wall. His heart beat in his throat. He crossed the room on tiptoes and tugged on the window. It held fast. No mechanism on either side to open it. He'd only get out of there if he smashed the pane. "Shit!"

He froze when he turned around. The hairs on his body stood on end. One of the girls sat bolt upright and stared straight at him. Her wide and glassy eyes locked onto his. A finger to his lips, he caught the shush before it left him. Her eyes were open, but her body still rocked with the rhythmic breathing of sleep. Whether he left with magnets or not, he needed to get out of there now. A child's bedroom should be their sanctuary. When had he crossed the line from a decent human being to a creep?

The door's hinges squeaked again, announcing Artan's exit. The lights were off on the ground floor and in the parents' bedroom. He ran down the stairs, his steps as light as his boots would allow.

"Yeargh!" The dad jumped from the front room and swung a baton at Artan.

Artan ducked. The baton hit the wall above his head with a *clang!* On the way up, he punched the man on the underside of his chin, the handle in his grip. The wet clop of a jaw being forced shut. The snap of teeth cracking together. The man's legs failed him, and he crumpled.

Shaking, Artan stood over him. But he didn't get back up again. Out of breath, his voice left his tight throat in a reedy whine. "I didn't want to do that. I just wanted to leave with some magnets. I didn't want to make you or your family feel unsafe." For what good it did talking to an unconscious man. An unconscious man who spoke a different language.

"Fuck it!" Artan dropped and rolled the man into the recovery position. The light from outside shone on his sprawled form. It also shone on a slim cupboard by the front door.

The cupboard door only a foot wide, but he should have seen it when he first came in. Artan pulled it open to reveal a column of three magnetic handles. He twisted each one free, one after the other, before shoulder-barging the front door open and slipping out into the night.

Artan ran around the side of the house and yelled when he bumped into Nick. "Shit! Nick, what are you doing?"

A bag in each hand, Nick said, "I got two magnets. Did you get any?"

"Three."

Nick held his bag open for him, and Artan dropped the magnets inside. "That's twenty-three," he said. "Three each and a couple of spares."

"Are you okay?" Nick rested a hand on Artan.

"Yeah." Artan nodded. Talking wouldn't make him feel any better about what he'd just done. His entire body trembled with the adrenaline dump. "Now let's get out of here. This place isn't doing my blood pressure any good."

CHAPTER 5

Olga's own reflection lay over the vile beast's face. She stumbled backwards, caught the back of her right ankle on a lip on the uneven floor, tripped, and landed on her arse. The shock of hitting the ground ran up her spine and culminated in a balled ache at the base of her neck.

She scrambled backwards, her feet slipping on the sandy floor. All the while, the creature watched her with its wide crimson glare. Olga reached the back wall. She pressed against the damp stone behind her to help her stand and drew her sword, the unsheathing steel resonating with the tone of liberation.

Matilda and Hawk stood beside her. Matilda armed with a sword, Hawk with his knife. Spears had no place in such close quarters. All three of them paused, pinned to the wall by the diseased's hatred.

"What do we do?" Matilda said.

Olga said, "Well, it isn't leaving anytime soon."

Hawk pointed his knife at the window. "Let's take a moment. It's not coming through the window, and the door's bolted. We need a plan."

"A plan?" Olga shook her head. "We kill it and be done with it. What more do we need than that?"

A shriek on their right. Olga spun toward the small corridor leading to the two bedrooms. Matilda's torch revealed another pair of bleeding eyes staring in through the window at the end. Fresh blood glistened in its glare. Like so many of the diseased this close to the wall, it wore the signs of the recently turned. Its broad frame suggested a formidable foe rather than some of the atrophied wrecks they'd fought in the north. It licked the glass. The pressure against the pane spread its fat tongue wide like a squashed slug. Its teeth caught the window with insistent clicks. But they had time. The diseased couldn't chew thr—

Bam!

The diseased at the living room window slammed an open palm against the glass.

Adrenaline lifted the hairs on the back of Olga's neck. She bounced on her toes. "So much for having time."

Bam!

The creature at the end of the hallway did the same.

Bam!

The sound came from one of the bedrooms.

"One of those windows is gonna break," Matilda said. She stamped her foot. "Shit! I thought we were well hidden in here."

They were well hidden. And then Olga gave them away. Sure, the diseased might have found them anyway, but she couldn't distance herself from their current predicament. "We need to take control of this."

"And how do we do that?" Hawk said.

Bam!

The first diseased attacked the window again.

Olga pointed at the locked door. "We open up. We funnel them in through the door. That way, we control the flow, and hopefully the windows won't get smashed in. We're going to have to fight them anyway. Hawk, that knife's useless. You open the door, and we'll take them down as they come through."

Hawk ran to the door and held the bolt.

Bam!

The first diseased hit the window so hard it left a diagonal crack along it.

Hawk said, "You ready?"

"No." Matilda shook her head.

Bam!

Another diseased attacked one of the bedroom windows.

Matilda shrugged. "But what else can we do?"

"Make sure you lean against the door," Olga said. "This will work if we only let them in a few at a time." She moved ahead of Matilda, ready to face the creatures as they entered. They wouldn't be in this situation were it not for her. She'd bear the brunt of it. She widened her stance and pointed her sword, tip first, at the door. "Okay, when you're ready."

Leaning his shoulder into the door, his feet planted, his stocky frame behind his pressure to prevent them from throwing it wide, Hawk freed the bolt with a *clack!*

The creatures outside fell silent.

Hawk opened the door by an inch. A rustle of leaves and snapping twigs swirled around the outside of the house. The beasts descended on them. Blind to their approach, Olga stared with unblinking eyes at the small gap in the door.

Thud!

The attack forced the gap wider and nearly knocked Hawk over. He grunted, and his feet slipped on the sandy floor. Arms stretched into the cottage. Their hands opened and closed as they grabbed at thin air.

"Yeargh!" Hawk threw his weight against the back of the

door, slamming the arms in the closing gap. The creatures withdrew. The outside lit up with their hellish shrieks.

"You ready?" Hawk's cheeks puffed with his deep breaths.

Olga glanced at Matilda, who nodded.

Thud!

A rush of diseased slammed into the door. The house shook, Hawk fell to the ground, and they flooded in.

CHAPTER 6

"Get down!" Gracie slammed into William, dropping her spear before she tackled him to the ground.

"What th—"

Gracie clamped her hand across his mouth. He twisted and writhed beneath her, but his scowl lifted when she pressed a finger to her lips.

They lay on the soft and damp ground, hidden by the three-foot-tall grass. The moon gave the grey clouds a backlit glow, like the monitors in the surveillance room. The monitors that had foretold Dout's collapse and the deaths of so many people she cared about. Lives that didn't need to be lost had she done the right thing and called out Max's behaviour.

An uneven gallop closed in on them. Heavy. Uncoordinated. Driven on by the wheezing and phlegmy rattle of clogged lungs.

A diseased passed them on their right. They were about twenty-five feet away. Too far to see them.

Gracie remained on top of William, her hand still

clamped across his mouth. She raised her eyebrows, and the tension slid from him, his body softening beneath her. She rolled clear and lay on her front in the damp grass, keeping her head low.

A second diseased followed. Slightly closer to them than their friend, but still at least fifteen feet from Gracie and William. Like every one of the vile things, it had two speeds: shambling when they were yet to sense prey, and then this. Although, what were they chasing? The creature leaned forwards while she ran, sprinting to catch up with her own failing balance. Her thick greasy hair hung down either side of her face in matted clumps. Her dark skin, puffy, swollen, and streaked with cracks like the top of a baked loaf.

As often happened with a pack of diseased, the front runners led the charge. Several at the head of the group, but the crowd was coming. Another diseased flashed past. Then two more, the closest still over ten feet away. An ache at the base of Gracie's skull from where she lifted her chin to watch them pass. Their thundering stampede ran pulsing vibrations through the ground.

The squall on Gracie's left spiked her pulse. A diseased passed on that side. Shit! They were surrounded. This one about six feet away. How long before one ran right over them?

Gracie reached for her spear, and William gripped his sword. More diseased passed on their left and right. Maybe twenty so far, and with no sign of the numbers thinning. Too many to fight. But if they had no choice …

A squall … flailing arms … its mouth open wide … the creature's feet planted with slamming steps before it fell. It hit the ground knees first, the violence of its landing snapping through it and catapulting it into the grass. It fell five feet to their left. Closer to William than Gracie.

The creature pushed against the ground with shaking arms and lifted its head. It supported the weight of its upper body in a kneeling press-up. A once-man, he had a thick and dirty beard. He still had many of his teeth. A deep gash ran down the right side of his nose. Like a dog watching its owner leave it behind, he stared after his pack. His jaw hung wide, his dried crimson stare vague, blinded by coagulation. More creatures passed on the left and right.

William's hand twitched. The glint of his shifting blade caught the moonlight.

The diseased turned their way, and Gracie snapped rigid. The thunder of more passed.

Gracie reached across with a shaking hand and covered the spot on William's sword where the moon reflected from its shiny surface. He lifted his weapon against her press, but she pushed down harder.

The diseased continued to stare in their direction.

Gracie's heart pounded against the ground. Her attention split between the diseased and William. Which one would screw her over first? She raised her eyebrows at her friend, the only effective form of communication with the creature so close. He had to trust her. If they needed to fight, she'd let go.

Fewer diseased passed on either side. Fewer, and they were farther away. The fallen creature turned its attention back to the pack. Its shaking arms wobbled as it forced itself to stand. Would they hold out long enough for it to get to its feet?

Crack!

Another creature slammed into him. The pair stumbled and fell several feet farther away from Gracie and William.

William's cheeks swelled from where he blew out. He dipped Gracie a nod. "Thank you."

She returned his gesture. "Thank you for trusting me. We couldn't win that fight."

Both diseased clambered to their feet like a pair of infirm, intoxicated geriatrics. The rest of the creatures had now passed. The two stragglers leaned forwards like they needed their imbalance to drive them on, and ran after their friends.

CHAPTER 7

The dewy grass had soaked the front of Gracie's clothes. But better soaked than dead. Previously, the wind tearing across the meadow had stung her sore eyes, adding to the itch of grief buried deep in them like sand. But now it also cut a chill to her core, her protective outside layer rendered redundant by the moisture. But they were alive. And they'd gotten away without a fight. With so many battles ahead of them, the more they avoided, the better.

"Thanks again for coming with me," Gracie said.

William shrugged, his brow furrowed from where he scanned their surroundings. They were just a minute or two from Dout's escape hatch. "I get it."

"What do you mean?"

"You have a chance to get something that belonged to your parents."

"But I'm risking my life for a trinket."

"Are you trying to talk me out of coming with you?"

"No." Gracie shook her head. "Just trying to understand why you're here."

William's voice faltered. He coughed into a fist. "Trinkets

become important when they're all you have left. Were I in your situation right now, if I had a relatively safe route back into Edin, I'd go back and get some things that belonged to my mum and dad. Something to remember them by."

The wind and the swish of the swaying grass filled the quiet between them. Gracie reached across and rubbed William's back. "They'll always be in your heart. In your memories."

"But what if they're not?"

"What do you mean?"

"Memories fade and change with time. What if the people I end up remembering aren't them?"

"Does it matter?"

William slowed to a halt. His eyebrows pinched in the middle. "Of *course* it matters."

"What I mean is, you only know people through your own perspective, which shifts with time. The same person can be many things to you over your life. So, with time, you would have changed how you saw them anyway. Additional information makes us view people in a different light. Even after they're gone. I've known many versions of my mum since she died. Even the ones I didn't want to know."

"Like how she could have been a better mum to Aus?"

The words formed a fist that slammed into Gracie's stomach. Her throat clamped, throttling her response. She turned her attention to the pile of diseased close to Dout's escape hatch. A small, unmarked grave off to the right. They'd not even had the time to write Max's name. Aus lay on his own where she'd left him. Where she'd killed him.

"He would have killed you had you not defended yourself," William said.

"How do you know?" Gracie shrugged. "Anyway, whether that's true, I still murdered him. There's no getting away from the fact. I killed him, and Dout fell because of me. I should have told my dad what I thought Max had done."

"What would that have achieved?" William said. "Didn't you say you weren't sure if they'd seen him?"

"But there was a chance they had. I should have played it safe."

"Playing it safe would have put us in danger. At best, your dad would have kicked us out. At worst, Aus would have killed us all. And what about the people of Dout?"

"What do you mean?"

"They would have all had to move somewhere safer. Just in case. Moving that many people would have attracted the attention of the diseased. The battle dragged them away, which at least gave those who survived a safe passage from here. Were I in your shoes, I wouldn't have said anything unless I was one hundred percent sure. What happened was Max's fault, not yours. Max is the one who should take the blame for putting you in that position."

"But he didn't know what he was doing. He didn't do it on purpose."

William halted again. He waited for Gracie to do the same before pressing his hands together, palm to palm. "Please afford yourself the same kindness you're showing Max. You had an impossible choice, and you tried to make the best decision."

"But people died."

"*Whatever* you did, people would have died. Max had already made that inevitable."

Gracie swiped the loose strands of her hair behind her ears. Her heart hurt. "Thank you, William." She turned towards the escape hatch. "Are you sure you're ready to enter Dout with me?"

"Of course."

The escape tunnel's hatch had a covering of rocks and

turf. Buried in the landscape unless you knew what you were searching for. Gracie tugged on the rock handle and pulled it open. "It looks smaller than when we left."

"I'm not surprised; we're about to climb down it blind," William said. "On the way out, it led to freedom. But at least we can't get lost down there. There's only one way to go."

Gracie kneeled on the edge of the two-mile-long tunnel and fought the tug of her own reluctance. She shoved her spear in first, the clack of the wooden shaft against steel echoing away from her. Far away. She slid in after it.

William followed and pulled the hatch shut, throwing them into total darkness.

Gracie's voice ran away from her. "I hope the others are doing okay."

"Me too," William said with a sigh. "Me too."

CHAPTER 8

"Yeargh!" Olga's cry tore at her throat as she ran to meet the first diseased's charge. She drove the tip of her sword into its soft face, spearing it like she'd done so many times before. It broke through the back of its skull with a satisfying *pop!* It turned the monster instantly flaccid.

Matilda stepped next to her, the diseased flooding into the small cottage. She stabbed through the cheek of one creature. Her blade angled up, it punched through the top of the diseased's head with an eruption of blood and bone.

The diseased outside fought to get in, sending a surge through the dense crowd. Olga kicked them back, temporarily slowing their progress.

But three slipped past and descended on Hawk before he had time to get to his feet. He fought them off from his back, kicking up at them and keeping them at bay. For now.

Olga shoved the diseased away a second time and followed with her sword. She stabbed one in the chest. A waft of rancid, rotten air hissed from the beast's lungs. Its mouth stretched wide. She'd robbed it of its scream. It fell back into the creatures behind.

Matilda spun away from Olga and hacked down one of the three looming over Hawk. She threw several wild swings, spraying the bare walls with blood.

The fallen diseased with the punctured lung lay across the doorway. Three more, forced forwards from behind and unable to get over their fallen brethren, tripped into the room and landed on the hard ground.

Two quick stabs ended two of them instantly. Olga stamped on a third, knocking it out before she ended it like the others. But more flooded in. And even when they fell, there were too many.

One last kick to drive the creatures back, the least effective one so far. Olga reached down for Hawk and dragged him towards the hallway leading to the two rooms while Matilda fought on his behalf.

Matilda backed in next to Olga. If they couldn't control the flow through the door, they could force them into a tighter space.

Shoulder to shoulder, Olga and Matilda defended against the onrushing diseased.

Sweat burned Olga's sore eyes. Matilda had dropped the torch, which threw an ineffective spotlight on the far wall. The darkness turned the creatures' black mouths and wounds into endless voids. But they didn't need to see any more than silhouettes. As long as they knew where their heads were. Rhythmic. Systematic. Olga and Matilda could do this in their sleep. The diseased would die before they ran out of energy. They executed them one after the next.

The increasing mound of bodies benefited them. A barrier between them and the enemy. Many tripped and fell. They made sure none of them got back up again.

Olga and Matilda stood in the hallway's entrance, gasping for breath. A pile of diseased in front of them. The creatures' foetid vinegar reek hung in the air like high humidity.

Tears ran down Olga's cheeks, and when she turned to Matilda, the lump in her throat robbed her of her words. It took several attempts before she squeaked, "I'm sorry," and then to Hawk, "I'm sorry."

Matilda's sword hit the floor with a *clang!* She threw her arms around Olga and pulled her close. "It's fine. It's been a hard time for all of us. We're here for you." She kissed her again and stepped back. Despite Olga bringing the diseased down on them, her eyes were kind and free of judgement. She flicked her head toward the fallen diseased. "At least they didn't break the windows."

Olga laughed through her tears. She pressed the back of her hand to her nose. "It stinks in here. Let's get these horrible bastards outside."

CHAPTER 9

His nose ruffled against the stink from the muddy ground and his elbows damp from pulling himself along, Artan crawled through the tunnel on his front, his bag of magnets beneath him to prevent them from sticking to the steel above. Out of the tight tunnel, he stretched up to the sky. A cloud passed across the bright moon, throwing a shadow over the dark landscape. Like Nick had done before him, he grabbed his spear sheath and slipped it over his shoulder.

"Well, that was much trickier than I expected," Nick said.

He hadn't knocked a dad unconscious in his own home. He hadn't left him on the floor in his front room for his family to find. But Nick didn't need to hear that. Not Artan's proudest moment. Sure, it was what he'd had to do, but still. "I'm just glad to be out of there."

"Right?" Nick said.

The weight of Artan's bag pulled on his shoulder. So when Nick tugged him back, he stumbled and threw his arms wide. "What are you doing?"

"We should check we have enough handles."

"You don't think we have enough?"

"If we don't, it's better we find out now while we can still do something about it."

The man in his home. The girl sleeping with her eyes open. He'd violated their private space. Every child had a right to feel safe in their own bed. Artan pointed at the wall. "I'm not going back in there."

"And hopefully we won't need to, but let's make sure, yeah?"

Artan dropped the heavy bag to the ground with a clatter. He hunched down and pulled three magnets from the cluster. Each of the three connected to the community's steel wall with a satisfying *clunk!* Two lower down, one for each foot. He attached the final one higher up, so they formed three points of a triangle. He stepped back.

Nick looked from Artan to the handles and back to Artan again. "What are you doing?"

"We need to check they'll hold us," Artan said.

Nick flicked his head at the magnets on the wall. "Go on then."

"But you're heavier than me."

"Are you calling me fat?" Even as he said it, an impish glint flared in his brown eyes.

"You're taller than me. You have a greater mass than me." Artan scanned the meadow stretching away from them. The cloud had passed, the moon highlighting the swaying grass. They'd see the silhouettes of the diseased before they got too close, but outrunning them in the open space with bags filled with magnets could prove tricky. "Can you just get on with it so we can get out of here?"

Nick winked at Artan, stepped onto the right magnet, grabbed the one at the top of the triangle, and then stepped onto the left. His mirth sank in time with his gentle slide down the wall.

"Shit!" Artan said. He twisted another magnet free from the clump in his bag as Nick jumped from the wall.

Artan attached another magnet between the two on the bottom. A line of three, he linked them by sliding his spear through their handles. "This should hold them together."

"You think three will be enough?"

"Those two you stood on moved slower than the one on the top. We need to have enough to hold you—"

"But not so many they become impossible to move up the wall."

"Exactly."

Nick pulled one of his own handles free from his bag and attached it higher up. One for each hand. This time, when he boosted himself from the footstep, he grabbed both handles. He clung to the steel wall and laughed. "It's working. It's holding me." He bounced up and down. The magnetic platform shifted a little. "Enough to stand on—"

"And to move them," Artan said.

Nick leaned away from the wall and reached in Artan's direction. "Hand me another magnet."

Artan twisted another handle free from his collection and passed it to Nick.

Thunk! He stuck it to the wall in between the other two, pulled a spear from the sheath on his back, and slid it through all three. Like he'd done with the ones at his feet, he pulled hard on them, snapping his body away from the wall from where he tried to disconnect them. Like with the ones at his feet, they shifted a little, but didn't come loose.

"You happy with that?" Artan said.

Nick held the shaft of his spear between the top magnets, braced against the wall with his feet so he no longer stood on the lower trio, reached down, and pulled the three he'd stepped on a little higher. He tugged on one side, lifting it by several inches before he brought the other side up to make the platform level. Standing on the now higher bar, he did the same with the top set. He shoved one side and then the other. "It's slow going, but I think it strikes the right balance. I can move them, and I think they'll remain stuck to the wall."

"And you don't think we can do it with any less?"

Nick hung from the top handles and pulled up those at his feet. A few inches higher, he said, "You try it."

Six more magnets, Artan took two spears and threaded three on each. He attached them to the wall. *Thunk! Thunk!*

"Shit!" Nick said.

"What?"

A few feet higher than Artan, he nodded back across the meadow in the forest's direction. "We've got some diseased coming this way."

"They've seen us?"

"They will if you don't get a move on."

Artan stashed his and Nick's bags close to the base of the wall and stepped onto the three lower magnets. He clung onto those higher with one hand, pressed his feet to the wall to take the pressure off the lower set, and pulled the ones he'd been standing on higher.

"They still coming?"

Nick squinted against the wind and nodded. "Yeah."

Slow progress, but it worked. Artan moved the handles above him higher, then pulled up the ones at his feet. One side at a time. Small gains, but gains nonetheless.

Artan drew level with Nick and ran his forearm across his sweating brow. The horde of diseased were at least forty strong. Breathless from the climb, he spoke through his gasps. "Any more than six magnets each will be too many."

Nick remained focused on the mob below. His shaved head and face glistened with sweat. "And any less will be too few."

"So that makes—"

"Forty-two magnets in total."

The diseased were now directly below them. Even from this high up, their rotten vinegar reek tainted the wind. He'd smelled it so often their stench became a paranoid memory that often hijacked Artan's senses, smothering him even when there were no diseased around.

The creatures moved like a pack of drunkards. They stumbled, bumped into one another, and squabbled. As the last of the mob passed, not a single one looking up, Artan said, "Forty-two's a lot of handles." How many more bedrooms would he have to sneak through? How many more people would he have to assault in their homes?

"We've got twenty-three, so it's less than we've already taken."

"But the next nineteen might not be as easy."

Nick shrugged. "Maybe we just need to go deeper into the community. And whatever it takes, we need to find a way. We won't get over the wall without them. And it's better we find that out while we can still do something about it."

The wind was stronger now they were higher up.

"You know," Nick said, "it's actually quite pleasant up here. We haven't had many times together where we can just be. With so much else going on, I'm going to take a moment while those bastards move on to enjoy this. What a view, eh?"

The strong wind. The dark meadow. The forest in the distance. One side of Artan's mouth lifted in a smile.

A few minutes passed, and the diseased were now far enough away. Artan unclipped the walkie-talkie from his belt and turned it on. The speaker belched an aggressive static hiss. He pressed the button on the side. "Tilly, it's me. Come in, Tilly."

"Artan?" Tilly spoke through her panting breaths. "Are you okay?"

Nick raised his eyebrows.

"Yeah, we're fine. Are you all right?"

"Yeah." She gasped.

"You don't sound it."

"I'd tell you if you needed to worry."

Nick shrugged.

"Okay," Artan said. "We've got about half the magnets we need. We're going back in to get the rest."

"Okay. Well done. Speak to you soon." The connection ended.

"What was that about?" Nick said.

"I'm not sure. But she'd tell me if they were having major issues. I'm sure we'll hear all about it when we get back."

"She wants us to focus on the task at hand," Nick said. "So let's do that."

The diseased vanished from sight over the brow of a small hill.

"At least we're no longer in Dout," Nick said.

"Huh?"

"Look." Nick pointed in the direction the diseased had gone.

"Damn," Artan said. An army on the move. They were much farther in the distance than the creatures. "There must be at least two hundred of them. You think they're going to Dout?"

"Why else would they be heading that way? The fight's over. They've won. They just need to secure their new base."

Artan blinked against the strong wind. Something about the sheer number of soldiers and the way they marched in perfect formation dropped a dead weight of dread through his stomach. "After that first battle, we wouldn't stand a chance against a second wave. Thank the heavens we got out of there in time."

CHAPTER 10

Like revealing a tomb, Gracie pushed open the hatch at the end of the escape tunnel. She crawled out into the pleasure dome and stretched her aching frame, pointing her fingers at the screened ceiling. The last time she'd been in here, it had been rammed with Dout's anxious citizens. Men, women, and children. They'd all grown used to the comfort and security of the community until she'd taken that away from them.

They'd left the underwater footage playing. A school of orange and yellow fish boosted past Gracie on her right. The reason for their startled movement swam into view. An alien of the deep, it patrolled the water like an invading spacecraft.

"What the …?" William's jaw hung loose.

"It's a giant squid," Gracie said. Long arms trailed behind it, longer and thinner feeding tentacles even farther back. It passed across the screens, temporarily blocking out the light from above.

"And I thought the diseased were scary." William's words died in the silent dome. Gracie had never known this place to be so quiet. The sky grew even darker as the squid passed directly above them.

Gracie shivered. "Come on." She tugged on William's arm. "Let's get moving."

William gently closed the escape hatch while Gracie went to the automatic door. She gripped her spear with both hands, leaned the tip towards the hallway, and waited for William to join her, his sword drawn.

Clack! She hit the button. *Whoosh!* The door slid open, announcing her and William's arrival to the ghosts wandering Dout's hallways. The lights brighter now they'd left the escape tunnel and pleasure dome. The glare itched Gracie's tired eyes. "It's never this quiet. Even when everyone's asleep." The steel walls took her voice and dragged the echo away from her around the circular corridor.

Gracie walked in front, past two of the eight tunnels leading from Dout. She glanced down them through the windows in the closed doors. They were both bright and unoccupied.

The next corridor was the one Artan and Nick had defended. Gracie pressed her face to the cold glass. The closest set of manual doors were partly closed. Spent ammo littered the floor. The second set of doors were shut, and the shields Hawk had dragged through lay nearby. The smoke-damaged windows obscured the diseased on the other side, so they were no more than meandering silhouettes. Diseased in her home. They were here because she'd screwed up.

"How long do you think they'll last down there?" William said.

Gracie coughed to clear her throat and threw her shoulders up in a shrug. "Who knows?"

"This isn't doing you any good," William said. "Let's keep moving."

They'd taken the long way around to her dad's room. No

matter what she'd done, Gracie had a responsibility to this place. What if there were still people down here? She checked the next tunnel, then the next, and the one after that. Each one stretched away from her. Empty. Stark. Bright. She froze before the next closed door.

William gave her a gentle shove. "Just walk past it. There's nothing down there for you now."

Except for her dad's body … The sacrifice he'd made because she'd screwed up. Gracie stumbled to the window and leaned against it. The first set of manual doors were closed, the glass smoky from her dad's explosion. It prevented her from seeing much beyond. Probably for the best. What could she do? Drag her dad's dead body for two miles down the tunnel and bury him in a meadow somewhere? He'd fallen with the place he loved. His entire life had been here. Including the memories of his dead wife.

"You okay?"

"No." Gracie shook her head. She bit her quivering bottom lip and sniffed against her running nose. "But I'm sure I will be with time." She stumbled away from the door. From the destruction she could have prevented. From the lives lost.

Whoosh! Gracie entered the dining hall. It looked even bigger with no people. Long gunmetal grey tables dominated the space, stretching away from them in neat rows. The bright light glistened off their rough surfaces, and they were covered with ceramic plates filled with half-eaten food. The plates in Dout were always empty because you only took what you needed and could always come back for more. But the people had lost their appetite for their last meal.

"You think there'll still be some food left?" William said.

Gracie led them through the tables towards the kitchen. "We're here, so we might as well check." She swallowed, her throat tacky, a stale taste lying on her tongue. "They'll definitely have water."

Usually, Gracie avoided the kitchen. She could go there whenever she chose, but the chefs were a territorial bunch. Outsiders didn't belong in their kitchen. Did they tell her how to run the surveillance room? Although, if they had, she might have done a better job. She scratched her brow with a shaking hand. "This is the first time I've come in here and the place hasn't been immaculate." Pots remained on the stove. They were crusty with old stew, the tomato sauce clinging to them like dried blood. Dirty plates spilled from the crowded sink.

Crash!

Driven by her pounding heart, Gracie spun on William with her spear, the tip just an inch from his throat. The steel pan he'd knocked over spun on the floor by his feet. He stood with his shoulders raised. "Sorry."

"Watch what you're doing."

William twisted even tighter. "Sorry."

They stored water in a large steel vat in the corner with a tap at the bottom. Before it went into the container, the kitchen boiled it to make it drinkable. Gracie swallowed a dry gulp, retrieved a small steel cup, held it beneath the spout, and turned on the tap. Some of the tension left her when the water filled the small receptacle. She handed it to William and filled another one for herself.

The stale water's familiar muddy undertones were even more earthy from where it had sat for nearly a day. But it quenched Gracie's thirst. She filled four water bladders and handed them to William before filling another four for herself. The kitchen always gave them half-filled bladders whenever they went out. They drank the contents while travelling and returned them full. Always bring back more than you take.

"Oh my!"

Gracie spun on William with her spear raised for a second time.

He hunched down in front of one of the large ovens, the door open. "They left some food behind." He pulled out a small pie and held it towards her in both hands, the top bronzed from where the pastry had fully cooked. William held it aloft like he'd picked up something holy. He pulled it back to his nose and sniffed. "Mmmm. Apple."

Her mouth watering, Gracie grabbed plates and cutlery before she followed William back out into the dining hall. He cleared a space for them at the closest table.

∽

"So where next?" Crumbs fell from William's lips to the steel top. When it became clear he wouldn't, Gracie fought the urge to wipe them from the surface. They didn't need to clean this place now.

Chewing her last bite, the fruit inside both sweet and sour, Gracie said, "I might eat more apple pies in this life—"

"Let's hope so," William said through his mouthful.

"But none will taste this good ever again. They say your favourite food is that which you were raised on." She took another bite. "This might be the start of a lifelong search to satisfy a nostalgic itch that can't be scratched." And maybe every mouthful from now on will have the same bitter taste of what she'd done to the people she'd been tasked with protecting. She took a sip of water. "The armoury's been looted, so there's no point in going there."

"So your dad's room?"

Gracie screwed the lid back on her bladder and got to her feet. "Yeah, let's go."

"It's small in here." William's mouth hung open as he turned a full circle in the centre of Jan's room.

"Dad always insisted on modest living. Especially after Mum died." Gracie forced her reedy words through her tight throat. Her dad had a bed, a shower, a wardrobe, and a small desk. "He wasn't the kind of leader who needed to remind the people of his power by having more than them. He ran this place with compassion and believed in equality." She'd destroyed his legacy with stupidity.

"That came across," William said. "Even in the short time we were here."

The desk had a drawer on one side. Like most things in Dout, it had been made from brushed steel, the action of the small drawer gritty from the friction of the finish. Gracie pulled it wide, shook her head, and leaned on the desk to support her sagging frame.

"What?" William said.

She pursed her lips. "They're not there."

William peered over Gracie's shoulder into the empty drawer. "Where are they?"

"I thought they were here." She shook her head. Her pulse quickened. Her lungs tightened. "I thought they'd be here for sure."

Gracie pulled clothes from her dad's wardrobe. She checked the pockets of each garment before she tossed them to the floor.

William had turned the mattress over, and he checked the bedsheets. A pile of clothes and bedding in the centre of the room. He added to it with the last pillowcase and winced when she looked at him. "I'm sorry."

"Fuck it!" The end of the word snapped like a whip-crack around the now silent room.

"We need to get out of here," William said.

"No!" Gracie shook her head. The room blurred through her tears. "No!"

"We can't stay here. We need to get back to the others. We tried."

"Not hard enough."

"Come on." William tugged on her arm. "You know there's nothing more we can do."

Gracie turned away from him, yanking herself free. "You go."

"Gracie, what do you hope to achieve by staying here? We need to leave. I'm sorry we didn't find the rings, but we tried. That has to count for something."

"It counts for nothing unless we find them."

"At some point, one of the armies who attacked us will come down here."

"Not in the middle of the night."

William grabbed her again and tugged harder.

Gracie resisted at first, but she soon loosened and let him lead her from the room. The *whoosh* of Jan's door called through the abandoned community.

William turned right, but Gracie turned left. He called after her, his voice echoing in the circular hallway. "Where are you going?"

"Dad might have them on him."

"*What?* You can't go down there. And if he had them on him before the explosion, who's saying he'll still have them on him now? It's carnage in that tunnel."

William's voice faded from where she left him farther behind. "I have to check."

"Shit!" William ran after her. "Fine. But just for the record, I think it's an awful idea."

CHAPTER 11

Gracie entered the tunnel with her dad in. Her movements were stilted from where she fought her own reluctance. She closed in on the door they'd manually locked, the wheel protruding from the wall. Like everything else in Dout, they'd abandoned it in a hurry. Like the lives that had been built and nurtured. The lives that she'd destroyed. She had to face her dad. Had to look upon his corpse and accept her part in his death. Aus had had every right to hate her.

Residue from the explosion coated the door's window, but it didn't prevent Gracie from seeing her dad's charred corpse when she pressed her face to the glass. A once noble man, he now lay on the ground like burned debris, blackened and ravaged.

"There are diseased down there." William stood at the window of the door beside her. The next set of manually operated doors were open. Forced wide by the attacking army. "Those creatures took down the soldiers your dad's explosion didn't reach. I thought they might still be here." He snorted an empty laugh. "It's not like they can climb back out again."

"And you didn't think to tell me?"

"That would have stopped you from coming here?"

Gracie kept her face pressed to the window, the condensation from her own breath reducing her visibility further. "They're down the other end. Near the ladders. Maybe I ca—"

"See what I mean?"

"I can sneak in there, check Dad's body, and get out again."

"I don't think that's a good idea."

"It won't be the first poor decision I've made."

"So you're ready to die for this one? What would your dad say?"

Gracie clenched her jaw and spoke through gritted teeth. "What do you know?"

"I trusted you in the meadow. I lay on my belly while surrounded by diseased. You need to trust me now."

"What are you talking about?"

"This is a fight you can't win. Those diseased will see you, and then you're screwed."

A lump had swollen in Gracie's throat since Dout fell. A tumour of grief that made it hard to breathe. She gulped against it and blinked, but her tears kept coming. Her rasping words ripped her throat. "I need to get those rings. I've lost everything. Everything, William. At least you still have Matilda. Those rings are *all* I have left of this life."

Thunk!

It came from the far end of the tunnel.

Thunk!

Another one. It landed like a lightning strike, shaking the ground when it touched down. A suited soldier dressed in a steel suit, they wore a helmet with a clear visor.

"What the fuck?" William said.

Thunk!

A third landed beside them, jumping from the ladder before they reached the ground. The first one pressed their thumbs into the eye sockets of the closest diseased. Blood squirted from the thing's face like juice from a squeezed tomato. It painted the front of the soldier's helmet.

Thunk!

"That's four of them now," William said. "How many more are there?"

"All right!" Gracie said. She sniffed against her running nose. "I get it. Let's go before they see us. Time to give up on the rings."

Gracie stumbled from one step into the next. Back into the circular hallway, she followed William while shaking her head. She'd screwed up again.

Whoosh!

The surrounding doors opened in stereo. The corridor on Gracie's left had been empty, but soldiers now climbed down the ladder at the end.

"They've found a way in," William said.

"And someone's used the controls in the comms room to open all the doors at once. We have to get them closed again before we're overrun." She took off, William pressing his back to the wall to let her past.

Crack! Gracie hit the button outside the comms room. The door opened, and she charged in, spear raised.

Two soldiers. Both of them wore the thick steel armour of the ones who'd entered the tunnel with the diseased. Both of them had removed their helmets and placed them on the side.

Gracie lunged at the one closest to her, driving the tip of her spear into his right eye. It sank with a squelch, and when she pulled it away, the soldier dropped.

William speared the second one with the tip of his sword. She went down like a diseased.

The control desk was bent and buckled, a heavy club lying on the floor from where the two soldiers had attacked it. Gracie pressed the button to close all the tunnels' doors. Repeatedly. It came loose and fell to the floor with the light tinkle of plastic against steel. "Shit! I can't close the doors. They're coming in whether we like it or not." The screens showed the soldiers above ground. They queued at every entrance while those at the front climbed in like wasps hijacking a hive. A walkie-talkie close by. "They must have co-ordinated it all from in here."

"We're screwed!" William said.

Gracie nodded. "Yep."

CHAPTER 12

They'd emptied their bags outside the community, leaving Artan and Nick carrying just one magnetic handle each. They gave them access to all the buildings in the place. At least all the ones they'd encountered so far. Now they needed to find nineteen more. It might be a lot, but at least they could quantify it. And better they knew now than when they were trying to climb the wall.

Outside another modest two-story cuboid home. The lights were off. Artan leaned close to the downstairs window and peered into the darkness. Could he violate another person's private space? Sneak in while their family slept, knock them out like the coward he was, and leave? Hopefully, by the time someone found that man in the morning, they'd be well away from here.

"Clear?" Nick said.

Artan squinted, shrugged, and then nodded. "Clear?"

"You don't sound sure."

"That's because I'm not."

"Do you see any movement inside?"

"No."

Nick took off around the side of the house towards the front door.

The second he vanished from sight, a light flicked on inside. "Shit!" Artan dropped the two empty bags and sprinted after him. He rounded the corner just as Nick attached the magnet to the door with a gentle *thunk!* "Stop!"

Nick jerked his head back. "Huh?"

"There's someone in there. The lights have just gone on inside. We need to get out of here."

Nick twisted the handle free and followed Artan back around the side of the house. Artan scooped up both empty bags as he passed them. He led the way, putting several houses between them and the place they'd nearly entered.

They hid behind a house at least fifty feet away. A man stepped out from the building they'd nearly robbed. He wore slippers and a dressing gown. Too cold for just that. And he must have thought the same. A quick check around seemed to satisfy his curiosity. He returned to his home.

"We got lucky with that first run of houses," Artan said. Until the last house …

"Then we'll find more like them," Nick said.

"But how deep will we have to go into this place to do that? What happens if someone sounds an alarm and we get rumbled? We won't stand a chance if this community wakes up with us in the middle of it."

"So what are you saying?"

"I think we should try the communal buildings again."

"You think they'll be clear now?"

"It's later. So hopefully. Do you have a better plan?"

"No." Nick shrugged. "Where shall we go?"

"I have an idea," Artan said. He threw Nick's empty bag back at him.

∼

"The armoury?" Nick said. "We've been in there enough times already. I'm confident they don't have a stash of magnets."

"Not the armoury." Artan pointed at the hall on the other side of the road. "That place over there." The moon and cloudy sky reflected off the dark windows. "It looks quiet. And, chances are, there will be a few more magnets inside the communal buildings. Spares for the people using the place."

"Okay." Nick led them across the road towards the hall.

A few steps behind, Artan ran with a stoop and checked up and down the road. Most of the community would be asleep by now. And with an army descending on Dout, the military presence would be thinner than usual. They'd picked the best time to rob this place.

"There's nothing in there." Nick pulled away from the window.

Cupping his face with his hands, Artan leaned against the glass. A large empty hall. Nothing more. "Shit! Maybe we sh …"

Nick ran off. He snuck around the side of the hall, and Artan chased him. He continued towards another communal building. Three times the size of the one they'd just peered into. The long building stretched at least two hundred feet from end to end. Lights were on at one end. Nick ran to the other.

Artan caught up to Nick, who peered through the window into the darkened room. He nudged him and pointed. "There are lights on down there."

"But that's down there."

Artan replied to Nick's whisper with his own lowered tones. "Are you mad?"

"Look inside."

Like he'd done with the communal hall, Artan cupped his hands around the sides of his face and leaned against the window. There were two neat rows of magnets attached to the wall, close to the door. "There must be—"

"Thirty magnets in there?" Nick said.

"Right. But what are those things?"

"Beds."

"What?!"

Nick said, "They're beds."

"You think there are people in there?"

"I'm certain of it. But they look like they're sleeping. Look, I know this is high risk, but if we can get in and out of there, then we're done and can get back to the others."

"I dunno," Artan said.

"Why not?"

"What is this place? It looks like some kind of barracks."

"Not some kind of barracks." Nick shook his head. "It *is* a barracks."

"Fucking hell," Artan said.

"So." One side of Nick's mouth rose in a smile. "We're doing this?"

Adrenaline surged through Artan, and he shivered in the cold. "Fuck it."

Nick slapped Artan on the top of his arm and led the way. He ran on tiptoes around the side of the building. Lit by the moon, he bit down on his bottom lip, bracing against the magnetic pull of the handle when he attached it to the door with a gentle *thunk!* He opened it with a sharp tug, pulling it wide before twisting his handle free.

Artan held his breath and followed Nick into the thick stench of flatulence, body odour, and old shoes. Twenty to thirty beds. Every one of them hosted a sleeping form. The moonlight accentuated their silhouettes. Each soldier had a gun beside them. Grabbing Nick's arm, he hooked his thumb towards the door. They had to get out of there. They'd made a mistake.

But Nick twisted away from him. He stepped closer to the magnets. And maybe he had a point. They'd done the hard part, and if they could get the magnets and get out of there, they were done with this place.

The closest bed was about ten feet away. Artan and Nick were closer to the door. A head start that could be the difference between life and death. A head start that made the risk more tempting.

Falling in beside Nick, Artan dropped to his knees and opened his bag. Adrenaline turned him clumsy, his hands shaking as he took the magnets one at a time. If just one soldier woke up ...

The magnets found one another in the bag. Several attached with a gentle *thunk!* Damn near deafened by his own rampaging pulse, Artan scanned the room. But the soldiers continued sleeping.

Each magnet Nick twisted free ground against the brushed-steel wall. A small but grating scratch.

Eleven magnets, Artan sealed his bag, placed it to one side, and opened Nick's. He took the next magnet from him and slid it inside. He put the next one in, the tug of the handle a warning too late. It dragged the first magnet across to meet it.

Thunk!

Nick's shoulders snapped to his neck, and his eyes widened.

Artan grabbed the handles of both bags in his right hand. He placed the palm of his left against the floor, ready to boost himself to his feet and get out of there. He whispered, "Sorry!"

But the room remained still.

Nick shrugged. Should he continue?

Artan nodded. They were all in now. They were nearly done.

Nick removed two at a time, stuck them together, and handed them to Artan.

Crash! An opening door somewhere deep within the building.

They both froze again. Steps marched towards them.

Nick quickened his pace, snapping the handles together in pairs.

Two more.

Then two more.

The steps continued to close in on the dorm.

Two more, Nick pulled the final two free and handed them to Artan.

While Artan sealed the second bag, Nick took the first. He halted. "Shit!"

"What?" Artan said.

Nick nodded at the door. "It's fallen shut. We should have put something in the way so it stayed ajar."

The door at the other end of the dorm opened. Nick grabbed Artan and dragged him out into the night, shoulder barging their way out of there while three men strode in and shouted in a language Artan didn't understand.

The building lit up as they left it behind, the glow shining after them like a searchlight.

Nick led the way across an expanse of asphalt. He ducked around the side of the closest building and pressed his back to the steel wall. He waited for Artan to pass him before peering back at the barracks. "That was close."

"Too close," Artan said. "But—" he raised his full bag and shrugged "—high risk …"

"High reward," Nick said. He slipped the straps of his bag over his shoulders, clapped a hand on Artan's arm, and said, "Now let's get out of here before they realise what we've done."

CHAPTER 13

The external wall might have only been twenty feet tall, but it still loomed large, stretching away from them in both directions. It appeared all the taller because the community dipped in the centre like a bowl, forcing Artan and Nick to escape on an incline. The parts of this place Artan had seen showed him the taller buildings were in the centre, the lower ground accommodating the more formidable constructions. Maybe they'd designed it that way to keep them hidden from the wall. Although, if they could see the wall from here, surely the wall could see them. Maybe they wanted to remain hidden from everyone else.

The part of the wall that stretched away to Artan's right curved in, obscuring his view of a large section of the community.

They approached the gap between the dog pen on their left and the small supply hut on their right. Close to their tunnel out of there, Artan let some of the tension fall from his tight frame.

"Why didn't we go to that place sooner?" Nick said. He

walked with a swagger. High risk, high reward. They'd taken it to this community and won.

"Because we needed to be desperate to try a stunt like that."

The community still sleeping, even their whispers threatened to carry on the wind. Nick laughed. "That's fair. I'm just glad to get out of here. Were you keeping count of the magnets? Please tell me you were?"

"Of course," Artan said. "We have twenty-one more. Forty-four in total. Two more than we need. We're golden."

Voices to their left. Nick spun to Artan, his face slack. He pointed at the dog pit. They were in there. Shit!

Artan ran for the small supply building, and Nick followed.

Around the back of the hut, and hopefully hidden from sight, Artan gripped the lip of the roof, pulled himself up, and attached his bag of magnets to the top. He continued to hang down, took Nick's bag, and put it next to his own.

Back on the ground, Artan copied Nick and drew his knife.

The people's voices left the dog pit and closed in on the small hut. They approached the door around the wall to Artan's right.

"Isn't it a little late to be tending to the dogs?" Nick said.

"Maybe the army uses them?"

"I didn't see any dogs from the wall, did you?"

"Maybe we didn't see them all. Maybe—"

A short man burst around the left side and slammed a steel baton over Nick's head. As Nick slumped, the man jumped over him and swung for Artan.

Artan ducked, and the baton rang when it hit the hut above his head. Backing away from the man, his knife in his right hand, he unclipped the walkie-talkie at his belt. "Tilly! Help us. We've been caught. Help—"

Artan dropped both his knife and his walkie-talkie. The man had at least fifteen soldiers behind him. They all carried guns. One of them dropped to bind the hands of the unconscious Nick. The others closed in on Artan. Their guns raised, they watched him down their barrels.

"Shit!" Artan raised his hands above his head.

CHAPTER 14

"What a lovely gift for the others to return to," Olga said. The last to enter the cottage, she closed the door behind her and slid the bolt into place. All because she'd screwed up again. She'd not controlled her emotions. She'd made too much noise and dragged them into a fight they didn't need or want. "Eighteen dead diseased on the doorstep."

Hawk snorted a laugh. He sat on the floor, leaning against the bare stone wall.

"You think that's funny?"

"Sorry, but it sounds like a ballad for our times. A little ditty about survival." He broke into song while pretending to play a mouth organ. "Wellllll ... I got eighteen dead diseased on my doorstep; there'll be eighteen more tomorrow. I've got eighteen dead diseased on my doorstep; there'll be eighteen more tomorrow."

Matilda cut in, "Eighteen down, but there's more in town. I got eighteen dead diseased on my doorstep."

Olga smiled at the laughing pair. "You two are batshit, you know that?"

"How else will we survive in a place like this?" Matilda said.

"I suppose." Olga sighed. "So what do you want to say to the others about what happened here?"

Hawk stretched his chin to the ceiling and scratched his scarred neck. "What is there to tell them? We live in a world filled with diseased. Some of them turned up. We killed them. End of."

Matilda straightened where she sat. She and Hawk had found one of the few patches on the sandy floor not soaked with diseased blood. She burst into song again. "We kilt them all 'til they dead. Stabbed a knife right through their head."

Hawk pointed at her and laughed. "We've got eighteen dead diseased on the doorstep."

Smiling again, Olga said, "Thanks, guys." It didn't take away from the fact that she'd screwed up, but at least she still had some friends left in this world. "You're kinder to me than I was to Max."

"What are you talking about?" Matilda said.

"When Max was at his lowest, I should have supported him. Instead, I let him know how he was holding us all back. Instead of hugging him, I told him to sort his head out." Her bottom lip trembled. "He wouldn't have gone outside Dout had I not. It's my fault Dout fell."

"That's bullshit, Olga," Matilda said.

"No, it's not."

"Look, I get what you're saying, and we could have all been kinder to Max, but he made the choice to go outside the community, not you. You were frustrated. We all were. And this life's intense. You weren't the only one who wanted to leave."

"I made it pretty clear that I wanted out of there too," Hawk said. "In fact, in the end, you were the only one who agreed to stay with him to give him the time he needed. We have enough to deal with; you beating yourself up about something you can't change won't help anyone."

"Yeah, maybe—"

A hard static hiss burst from the walkie-talkie on the window ledge. Matilda ran to it, snatched it up, turned the volume down, and pressed it to her ear. Her mouth hung open while she listened.

The walkie-talkie spluttered, parts of words delivered between bursts of disconnection. "Hu-fa-don't-help-mu-jow."

"What the fuck does that mean?" Olga said.

"That's Artan." Matilda focused on the walkie-talkie, her eyes seemingly unable to fix on one particular spot. She shifted her weight from one foot to the other. "He's in trouble."

"How can you tell?" Hawk said.

"I'm not sure."

"Well, I dunno about anyone else"—Olga stood up—"but if we think they need us, we need to get over there." It had to be better than waiting in the cottage for more diseased to arrive.

The walkie-talkie still in her hand, Matilda chewed on her bottom lip and raised her eyebrows at Hawk.

"Sure." Hawk shrugged. "It's the only thing we can do."

Olga handed Hawk the torch. "Shine this on the wall, will you?"

The bright beam lit up the back wall. The sandy floor had stones and twigs around the edges from where parts of the forest had found their way inside. Olga picked up a sharp piece of flint about two inches long, her arm shaking with the pressure of scoring her message into the wall.

"Gon to hep Artan and Nick. Be brack spoon?" Hawk said.

"I can't spell in capitals, all right?" Olga returned to her message and fixed it. "Better?"

One side of Hawk's mouth rose in a smirk, and he winked at her.

Olga took the torch back. "You ready to go?"

"What are you doing with that?" Hawk said.

"Whoever gets back here will need it the most. The second we leave the forest, we'll have the moonlight to guide us."

"But we've got to get through the forest first."

"I'm leaving it here in case any of the others get back before us. How else will they see the message?"

"So we're going to go back through the forest in the dark?"

"You're what, twenty-one?"

"Twenty-three. At least I think I am. Birthdays have never been that important to me, and I've kind of lost track. What's your point?"

Olga placed the torch on the window ledge. "My point is, aren't you a bit old to be scared of the dark?"

"It's not the dark that scares me. It's what's waiting in it."

Olga shrugged. "I get what you're saying, but we're leaving the torch. We'll be out of the forest in no time, and then we won't need it. In fact, it'll just be something extra to carry."

Hawk's rounded shoulders and set jaw suggested the banter had left him. He nodded. "Okay. Fair enough. Now let's see what trouble Artan and Nick have gotten themselves into."

CHAPTER 15

The suit doubled Gracie's weight, and her shoulders rounded beneath the burden of the steel armour. Beneath the burden of what she'd done to her home. She'd turned a safe community into hell on earth because she thought she knew best.

The helmet reeked of someone else's stale breath, and the grimy visor tinted Gracie's view of her community. But at least the suit had room for her and her four filled water bladders. She gripped her spear in a gloved hand while William held his sword.

"You ready?" Gracie flinched as her voice bounced back at her.

William's transparent visor framed his blank face.

"I said are you ready?" Louder this time.

William remained vacant.

Gracie pointed at the door. "That way?" She turned her palms to the ceiling. "What do you think?"

William nodded.

This would get old fast.

Within three steps, Gracie's breathing grew heavy and

sweat itched beneath her collar. These suits struck a fine balance. They were thin enough to wear, but thick enough to be worth wearing. No rotting teeth could chomp through her steel outer layer, but she wouldn't be running any marathons in it any time soon.

Gracie slammed a clumsy palm against the door's button, and it slid aside, the familiar whoosh of the action muted because of the suit. Her legs already aching, she left the room with slamming steps. Her spear and William's sword might mark them out as someone who shouldn't be in the suit, but who was to say she hadn't picked it up when she'd entered? And they only needed the other soldiers to hesitate for a moment for them to have the advantage.

The door to the first tunnel on their right was open. At least fifty soldiers gathered around the bottom of the ladder at the other end. They stared up at those coming down to meet them.

About twenty soldiers burst from the next tunnel ahead. Gracie tensed when they raced towards her. She tightened her grip on her spear.

But they charged straight past and entered a communal dorm behind them with their guns raised. Their mouths flapped from where they shouted. Being preoccupied with clearing every room in the place had made Gracie's spear and William's sword invisible.

The pleasure dome on her left, Gracie hit the button to open the door. "Shit!" The echo in the helmet agreed.

Fifty to one hundred soldiers in the domed room. Another underwater scene played on the screens. A tropical environment, stingrays glided through the water, disturbing seahorses and shoals of brightly coloured fish. Many of the soldiers watched the scenes with their jaws hanging loose.

The words were wasted on William, but she said them

anyway while gesticulating her intention. "We're going to go back outside. I need you to follow me, okay?"

William's helmeted head dipped with a slow nod. Gracie returned a raised thumb, and she left the room.

More soldiers flooded in from the open tunnels. They ran with intent. They had a job to do and somewhere to be.

Sweat from Gracie's brow stung her eyes. She strode with the purpose of someone who belonged. The purpose that had always driven her confident steps in this place. She and William had somewhere to be. They didn't have time to engage with the soldiers.

They reached the tunnel Artan, Nick, Hawk, and Freddie had defended. The first set of manual doors were still closed, and their grimy windows obscured what waited on the other side until she got to within a few feet of the glass. Heat prickled her skin. One to two hundred diseased in her home. The grime on the windows consisted of a mixture of blood, saliva, and pus. Crimson eyeballs glared at her. Piggy noses squashed against the window. Teeth chinked against the glass.

Four people in steel suits much like Gracie's and William's gathered at the other end of the tunnel near the base of the ladder. They worked their way through the creatures. They carried swords and spears, much like her and William. Maybe the gloves were too thick for triggers. Or the space too tight for bullets.

William grabbed the wheel to open the door, and Gracie gave him a thumbs up.

The split down the centre of the doors opened by an inch. Long and bony fingers stretched through. Ten to fifteen diseased, they hooked onto the doors and pulled at them as if they could aid William.

The suited soldiers continued to fight, occupied by the task at hand.

Gracie backed against the wall when the gap in the doors opened to about a foot. The first diseased stumbled through, its mouth stretched so wide its teeth pointed forwards. It only took one to topple a community, and they were about to send through many more than that.

William still spun the wheel. The gap widened, and the diseased spilled from the space in ones, then in twos and threes.

One of the suited soldiers pointed down at them. "Shit!" Gracie said. "They've seen us." She tugged on William's arm and pointed for him to see.

The soldiers ran towards them. More diseased tore past, their shrill fury muted by Gracie's suit.

They'd already let over fifty diseased through. Enough to topple Dout. It only took one. As many as they'd let through, if not more, queued at the gap. The press of bodies slowed the suited soldiers. They dragged back the creatures and tossed them aside.

Gracie circled her hand anticlockwise in front of William's face. "Close the door!"

William flicked into reverse, the doors closing on the diseased while she stabbed through the gap, her spear sinking into the stomach of the first beast. It pulled back, slowing the advance of several creatures behind it.

Gracie met the second surge by jamming her spear into the face of the next creature. The tip burst through the back of its skull and dropped it. Those behind clambered over the diseased corpse and charged into Dout.

Pulling the dead diseased clear, Gracie dragged it through to their side while William continued spinning the wheel.

The suited soldiers hacked and slashed in their desperation to reach Gracie and William. They were still about twenty feet away and had been slowed to a near standstill.

The gap in the door now only about a foot wide, Gracie

sent back as many creatures as made it through. She stabbed stomachs and legs. Blood pooled on the floor, but the muting effects of the suit detached her from the horror of her reality. No ear-splitting shrieks. No rancid vinegar rot.

The gap about a foot wide. The suited soldiers fifteen feet from the doors. William moved with a mechanical efficiency befitting his appearance. He spun the handle, and Gracie stabbed the diseased.

If motion equalled progress, the soldiers would have reached them by now. Frantic in their battle to get through, but the thick crowd proved almost impassable. Like someone who couldn't swim being dropped into the middle of a lake, the suited soldiers flailed. Slashing and stabbing, they got absolutely nowhere. They were drowning in diseased.

William twisted his entire body, sealing the doors with a hard turn of the wheel. They locked the soldiers in on the other side. They stood amongst the diseased and watched Gracie and William like their crimson-glared comrades. Rendered impotent by the barrier between them, but no less furious. Gracie flipped them the bird, turned away from the window, and led her and William back out into the circular corridor. He'd trusted her this far. Hopefully, her plan would work.

The diseased tore through Dout. They charged around the circular corridor surrounding the pleasure dome and dining hall. They gathered outside the doors to the dorms. They knew people waited inside.

Gracie slammed her hand against every button she passed, opening the doors to each one. Bullets burst out of some of the rooms, temporarily driving the diseased back. But there were too many of the creatures. They might have lost those at the front, but the others flooded in, overrunning every space they entered. Closing in on her dad's room, she wagged a finger at William. Not this one.

A crowd of diseased gathered outside the pleasure dome. Larger than any other group, they leaned against the closed doors. Gracie shoved several aside and slapped the button to let them enter.

The creatures brought panic with them. Now close to eighty soldiers in the domed room. Not a single one of them wore a protective suit.

Some soldiers had guns. In the chaos, they shot anything that moved, taking down more of their own than they did diseased.

Ting! Gracie's pulse spiked when a bullet hit her visor. It left a black mark directly in front of her left eye. *Ting!* Another one bounced off her steel suit.

The gunfire stopped. The soldiers were down. The fury left the diseased. Nothing to attack here.

William opened the dome's door, and the creatures left.

Gracie removed her helmet and gasped. Dout echoed with cries and screams. Her eyes itched and her vision blurred. What would her dad say if he could see the state of the place now? And all because she'd covered up for Max. He'd be so disappointed.

"We don't have time to grieve," William said.

"I'm not!" Gracie rubbed her eyes.

William placed his helmet on the floor beside him. "We need to get these suits off and get into the escape tunnel. We … Wait!" He snatched up his helmet and pulled it back on.

Gracie copied him. She should have realised sooner.

Between thirty and forty downed soldiers on the floor around them. The suits hid the nuance of their current states. They weren't all dead. At least half of them twisted and twitched. They wobbled and swayed while getting to their feet. The doors to the pleasure dome remained open. The creatures left the room when their bodies allowed it, several of them slamming into the frame on their way out. Gracie winced when one hit it so hard the vibration of its impact shook through the floor. It spun like a top and fell out into the corridor onto its back. It twisted on the ground like a crushed spider, the other diseased trampling it as they left. It finally stood again, its greasy hair hanging down as it stumbled from sight.

Fewer bodies in there, but corpses and paralysed diseased still covered the floor. Blood leaked from the dead's visible wounds. William closed the pleasure dome doors, and Gracie worked through the writhing beasts. She stabbed her spear's sharp tip through the right ear of the first, moving along the line, shutting them off one after the other. William was right; they didn't have time to grieve.

Gracie removed her helmet for a second time. It hit the floor with a *clang*. She discarded her gloves next, and then the suit's top and trousers. Her sweat-soaked clothes clung to her. She flipped open the escape tunnel's hatch, retrieved her spear, and slid into the tunnel head first. A two-mile crawl in the dark. Again. And she hadn't found the rings. But at least they had water. Their trip hadn't been for nought. Although she wouldn't count it as anywhere near a victory either.

The light from the pleasure dome shut off when William closed the hatch. The tight tunnel amplified their panting struggles.

"For a minute there," Gracie said, "I wondered if we'd make it out alive."

"Tell me about it," William said. "I don't ever fancy doing that agai—"

Thunk!

The light from the pleasure dome flooded in through the end of the tunnel.

"What's ha—"

A diseased scream cut off Gracie's question.

The furious face of a creature appeared. And then its

shoulders. It twisted and fought as if being boiled alive. Steel-gloved hands forced it into the tunnel. The diseased stopped fighting when it fixed them with its crimson glare. Gracie's blood ran cold.

"Oh, shit!" William said. "Go! Now!"

CHAPTER 16

The darkness lifted, ripped away from Artan with the removal of the fabric hood. He pulled back from the face now inches from his own, the feet of his steel chair scraping across the concrete floor. Ropes across his lap bound him to the seat, his ankles were tied to the front chair legs, and they'd tied his wrists behind his back.

A line of strangers stood in front of him, and the room's bright lights were blinding. They were positioned on the floor around the room and shone directly into his face.

The only defence he had, Artan blinked against the glare. With every passing second, he made more sense of his surroundings. He sat in a box room that had glass walls on three sides. The left wall, the only one made from steel, had a closed door in it. The open roof revealed the cloudy night sky. They were higher than most of the community. He hadn't seen this place before. The dog-leg bend in the external wall must have hidden it from sight.

Around fifteen hundred houses below them, larger industrial buildings scattered throughout. Warehouses. Factories. Barns. The fields of their agricultural section over to his left. The dog-leg bend in the wall had hidden it all.

The lights on the ground lit up both Artan and Nick beside him. They'd put them on display as a hellish art installation for the people of this community to enjoy. But they'd have to wait until morning for most of the citizens to wake up before they were fully appreciated.

Like they'd done with Artan, they'd tied Nick to a steel chair. They'd bound his hands behind his back. Ropes around his lap tied him to the seat, and they'd strapped his ankles to the front chair legs. Unlike Artan, they'd beaten him so badly his head hung limp, and blood drooled from his mouth.

Six soldiers dressed in dark green uniforms lined up in front of them. Each of them held a gun in a two-handed grip. They glared at Artan and Nick. Just give them one excuse and they'd fill them with holes.

"Artan?" Nick slurred his words. He poked his tongue from his mouth and licked his cracked lips.

The soldiers watched on in silence. Did they understand what Artan and Nick said to one another? "Are you okay, Nick?"

Nick expelled a burst of red mist with his snorted laugh. "My head's a bit sore."

The soldiers' expressions remained unchanged. Surely they'd make it clear if they didn't want them talking.

"These are the lot who took Shah, you know?"

"Aus mentioned him briefly. He was one of Aus' runners, right? What exactly happened to him?"

"You don't want to know."

Artan held eye contact with one soldier. A man. The tallest of them all at well over six feet four. If anyone wanted to assert their authority, it would be him. "They killed him, right?"

No reaction from the soldier. He clearly didn't understand. Or he didn't care.

"Death would have been kinder than what they did."

Artan's stomach sank. "He's still alive?"

"Oh, no."

"What did they do?"

"You sure you want to know?"

Six armed soldiers. Every pair of eyes stone cold. "Y-yeah."

"They cut off all his fingers and toes. They skinned his feet and hands." Nick shook his head. "They stripped him naked and cut off his penis before they turned him loose."

At the mention of being dismembered, Artan twisted in his seat, the bonds preventing him from curling too far. "Shit!"

"By the time we found him," Nick slurred, and another wave of glistening crimson drool ran from his mouth in a stringy surge, "he was delirious, and his wounds were so infected there was nothing we could do to help. It's one of the many reasons Aus hated them so much."

If the soldiers understood Nick's words, they hid it well. "But why did they do it?"

"Who knows? We can't understand a word they're saying, and from what I can tell, they don't understand us either."

"Shit. Tilly's gonna come."

"You called her?"

"Yeah. I used the walkie-talkie before they captured me."

"And where's the walkie-talkie now?"

"I don't know. I dropped it and my knife when they pointed a gun at me. It didn't seem worth dying for."

Nick inhaled and straightened in his seat. His right eye had swollen shut, and his bottom lip opened at the front with a deep split. "I'm sorry, Artan. We shouldn't have gone into those barracks. It was a bad idea. I got greedy when I saw all those magnets."

Artan breathed in through his nose, his chest rising with his inhale. What could he say? They'd fucked up big time and now this: placed on a hill so the community could see their public torture and humiliation. He finally found the words and returned his attention to the soldiers in front of them. "It's happened. What we need to do now is work out how we can get out of here."

"I'm sorry."

"Dwelling on it won't get us anywhere. It won't rewind time. It won't undo *your* mistake."

"I'm—"

Snap! A door opened behind them.

Artan spun around, turning against his bonds' restraint. Another man in uniform entered. But, unlike the others, who wore green, this man dressed from head to toe in orange. The six soldiers lowered their gaze in unison.

The man stood about five feet six inches tall. Fat around the waist, he resembled a terracotta pot. His tanned skin glistened with sweat and grease like he moisturised with lard. He'd clearly lived a decadent life, but he seemed untouched by the joy that came with indulgence. His thin lips pulled tight, revealing his wonky and yellowed teeth. His black eyes were devoid of life. A small line of beard about half an inch thick ran from his sideburns and tracked his jawline, meeting up in the centre of his chin to form a goatee. Clearly no one had the stones to tell him how fucking ridiculous he looked.

A woman followed him in. She stood about a foot taller and had jet black hair tied in a ponytail so tight it lifted her thin eyebrows. Her skin shock white, she carried a brown holdall, the leather cracked with age. The true reason for the soldiers' averted eyes, they recoiled in her proximity. She walked around in front of Artan and Nick, dropped to her knees, and opened her bag.

First, she laid out a small black cloth like she might be about to set up a picnic. Two feet square, she took her time in straightening out the creases, each action deliberate and with the utmost care. She removed tools from her bag one at a time and laid them out in a regimented line. Bolt cutters. A rusty knife stained with blood. Razors. A long dagger.

"W-what are they?" Artan said. His chair legs cracked against the concrete from where he pushed his toes into the ground to move back. "What are you going to do?"

Nick's one open eye glazed when he fixed on the woman's tools.

The woman removed Artan's walkie-talkie from her bag and placed it down next. She pressed the button on the side, an angry static hiss bursting from the speaker.

"Artan?"

The woman pressed the button again for Artan to respond, but he bit his bottom lip. What would he achieve in having a conversation with her?

"Don't worry, peaches," Matilda said, "we're coming for you. We're heading to the front gate now. We'll find a way in."

"Shit!" Nick shook his head. "I hope they don't understand what she's saying."

The rattle of chains entered the room with a yelping man. Another soldier, he wore the same green uniform as the others. But he clearly didn't get the same privileges. Bald and in his mid to late thirties, he was so skinny Artan did a double take. He looked like one of the diseased. The chain had worn a red-raw hoop around the man's neck. He yelped again when the soldier leading him in yanked harder, standing him next to the torture weapons and the kneeling woman.

The man tugged on his chain collar and threw a sideways glance at the soldier holding the other end of the chain. He coughed to clear his throat and straightened his back like he could somehow rescue dignity from the jaws of humiliation. "I'm their translator."

"Translator?" Artan lifted one side of his mouth in a sneer. "You look like their fucking pet."

"I'd rather be standing here with a chain around my neck than tied to one of those chairs. At least I know I'm walking out of here. So, before we feel the need to cast any more aspersions, let me explain my role. I'm here to make sure they understand what you're saying."

"I know what the word *translator* means."

The translator sighed. "Combine that with what might come through on the walkie-talkie, and maybe you'll stay alive for longer than five minutes. Maybe even permanently. Certainly until the people on the other end of that radio arrive."

"Artan, I'm sorry," Nick said.

"That won't keep Matilda and the others safe, will it?"

The terracotta soldier shouted at the bald slave. "The general said you fucked up big time."

"It was my fault," Nick said. "I'm sorry."

The translator relayed the message to the fat little general.

"Because you broke into a resident's home," the translator said. "And knocked them out. Y—"

"What did you say?" Artan said.

"You broke into someone's home and attacked them. The general assumes you had something to do with the war we just fought, but he doesn't care about that. We've won. The place is ours. But what he does care about are the people of this community. They should feel safe in their own homes."

"That was me," Artan said. "I was the one who broke into their home and knocked them out."

"What?" Nick said.

"I didn't want to say anything. It's why I didn't want to go into the residential area again. I got jumped. I lashed out. I felt so ashamed, which is why I didn't tell you. I wanted to make sure he was okay. I left him in the recovery position …"

Nick's jaw fell slack, and more blood ran over his bottom lip. "So it was nothing to do with the …" He glanced at the translator with his one good eye. The less they said in front of him, the better.

"The man you knocked out was the one who alerted us to your presence. The general takes the safety of our citizens seriously. A child should be able to sleep in their own bed without fear."

"I agree," Artan said.

"What did you do to their kids?" Nick said.

"I hid in their room to avoid their dad. They must have seen me when I was in there." Artan glanced at the tools on the black blanket.

The general spoke. The translator translated, "Now we must punish you."

The general clicked his fingers, and two soldiers released their guns so they hung from their leather straps across their fronts. They stood on either side of Nick's chair and lifted it while another soldier opened the door in the steel wall, making way for them to carry him through.

The tall woman rolled up her black blanket with the tools inside, placed them back in her bag, and followed Nick and the others. She left the walkie-talkie behind.

Artan twisted in his chair. The ropes cut into his lap, but they loosened a little. "Why are you taking him?"

The general leaned close to Artan. He smelled like a sweating horse. His beady little eyes narrowed and his face reddened when he screamed, his translator delivering the message. "You screwed up. You hurt one of our citizens. That hurts me. If they suffer, I suffer. But it's too easy for me to punish you. Instead, your friend will pay the price for your error."

Crash!

The door between Artan and Nick slammed shut. A few seconds later, Nick howled.

CHAPTER 17

A shrill scream to the right sent a chill down Olga's spine and stopped her in her tracks. She turned in the noise's direction, clung to her sword, and like Hawk and Matilda beside her, pointed the tip of her weapon in the sound's general direction. When not obscured by cloud, the moon laid a silvery highlight across the perpetually moving carpet of long grass stretching out before them.

"I can't see anything," Hawk said. He clung to his spear. At least one of them had a weapon with range.

Matilda pointed her sword in the direction they were heading. "I say we get out of here. Going towards Artan will take us farther from them, anyway. And if we can't see them—"

"They can't see us," Olga said. "Good call." She led them away.

They crested the brow of a small hill, the community Artan and Nick had gone to ahead of them. The main wall formed an imposing horizon behind it. Their intended destination might have been home to thousands, but the main wall looked like it had been laid by the gods.

They closed in on the twenty-foot-tall steel perimeter. Olga and the other two scanned their surroundings. She frowned against the wind. "Unless the diseased are lying in the grass like snakes, we should have plenty of warning if they come this way."

Ten to fifteen feet from the wall, Hawk threw his arms up in a shrug. "So where are they?"

"Do you think it was just the walkie-talkie playing up?" Olga said.

Matilda moved closer to the wall. "I think it might be more than that." She pointed at the ground. "These must be the magnets Artan was talking about. He said they have about half of what they need."

"You think that's only half?" Hawk said.

Matilda shrugged. "If it's all of them, where are they now? I don't think they've come back out again since they first contacted us."

"Maybe they called us because they want a hand carrying them back?" Olga said.

"Maybe they ran into the army inside on their second run." Matilda pinched her bottom lip, and her voice grew higher in pitch. "Maybe they're trapped somewhere."

"That's a lot of maybes," Hawk said.

Matilda's eyebrows pinched in the middle. "Maybe that's a good enough reason for us to go inside?"

"Maybe," Hawk said. "Let's think about it for a moment. What do we know for sure?"

"They've brought some magnets outside," Olga said. "But we knew that, anyway."

The walkie-talkie hissed when Matilda raised it to her mouth. "I'll tell you what we'll do, peaches."

"What's with the peaches?" Olga said. "First Artan when you called him, and now me."

Matilda pressed her finger to her lips and continued to

speak into the walkie-talkie. "We're going to walk right up to their front gates and demand to be let in."

Olga waited for her to let go of the button. "You still think someone might be listening?"

"If they're not, Artan will have turned it off, so what harm can it do?" Matilda pulled the bush aside to reveal the tunnel beneath the wall. "I'm going in, and I want to make sure if there's a welcoming party waiting for us, it's waiting where we're not."

Hawk tilted his head to one side. "So we're going in?"

"*I* am," Matilda said. "I have to."

"What if they don't need our help?" Hawk said.

Matilda shrugged. "Then we'll come out again. I'm not prepared to leave it to chance. I can't stand here worrying about Artan. I'd rather make a wasted trip than find out my inaction led to him or Nick getting harmed."

Had Olga done all she could for Max, he'd still be here right now. "Matilda's right."

"Huh?" Hawk said.

"We don't know our best course of action, but what if Artan and Nick need us and we do nothing? At least if we go inside, we're trying to help. Besides—" she looked over one shoulder and then the other "—it beats waiting here for a diseased horde to show up."

Hawk picked up one of the magnetic handles.

"What's that for?" Matilda said.

"I have a plan. Come on, let's go."

CHAPTER 18

"Follow me," William said.
What else did he expect her to do? William ahead of her in the tunnel, the soles of his boots flipped one way and then the other from where he dragged himself forwards by his elbows. His clothes swished against the steel, and he grunted with the effort. They both moved as fast as they could, but the snarling, snotty rasp behind Gracie told her they weren't moving fast enough.

Sweat burned Gracie's eyes and dripped from the end of her nose. Her elbows throbbed. She slammed them down, one after the other, using them to pull herself away.

The snarling and growling drew closer. Every time Gracie looked back, the beast and its dark red glare had closed the distance between them. So what if her elbows were sore? If her eyes stung. Anything had to be better than the diseased latching onto her with its rotten and infectious bite.

"How you doing, Gracie?" William said.

"They're faster than us." Whoever sent in the first

diseased hadn't stopped there. The suited soldiers mined their plentiful supply, sending a steady stream after them.

The leading diseased opted for a different approach to propel itself along the tunnel. Instead of elbows, it pulled with its hands. It slapped its palms against the steel and dragged. *Slap! Swish! Slap! Swish!*

The vinegar tang caught in the back of Gracie's throat. A halitosis stench, driven towards her on the back of the beast's ragged pants.

Strapped up with water bladders and her throat so dry it stuck with every swallow. But Gracie had no time to drink.

Slap! Swish! Slap! Swish!

Every glance back slowed Gracie's escape. An excrement reek mixed with vinegar rot. The next one had drawn close enough to pollute her air. This tunnel belonged to the diseased. Give it time and they'd be in control of everything in it. They grew louder as they drew closer.

Slap! Swish! Slap! Swish!

Gracie winced the moment before every slapping hand hit the steel tunnel. The next one would clamp over the back of her ankle.

Slap! Swish!

It would drag her back, and the monster would smother her. Bite down on her.

Slap! Swish!

Gracie pulled her knees towards her chest.

"What are you doing?" William said.

The tip of her spear pointed up the tunnel in the direction they were heading. The shaft was too long to turn it around in the tight space. She spun and faced the creature behind. She lunged at it with the blunt end of her spear. It sank into its mouth with a wet squelch that dislodged several teeth. The tunnel amplified the beast's shrill scream.

Gracie's second jab squashed the thing's nose with a cartilage-crushing crunch. She grunted with the effort of her attack. More sweat poured from her. She poked it in the eye. One eye and then the next. She blinded the fucker, but it still came forwards. It swung its head. It bit at the air. Blood drooled from its mouth in thick strings.

"Here." William tapped her feet with the tip of his sword.

Gracie took his weapon, and he took hers.

One swift jab buried the sharp tip in its face, and it fell limp. Its forehead hit the floor. Blood pooled beneath it. A spasming hand slapped on the fallen diseased's back. The creature behind pulled itself over the top of its downed comrade.

Gracie slid back.

The next creature grunted, and blood from the ever-expanding pool splashed up from its hands. It slithered from its friend's corpse into the crimson puddle.

"Yeargh!" Gracie stabbed it in the face twice. The second stab killed it. Yet another diseased climbed over the first two.

Gracie shuffled back several feet and stabbed the next beast. She killed it on her first attempt and retreated again.

Killing the next one, Gracie pulled back and killed the next. A steady stream of the vile things followed her along the tunnel. How long could she keep this up?

"What are you doing?" William said when she stopped.

She waited for the next diseased to reach her, and killed it. Another stabbing lunge, her arm aching from holding the heavy sword parallel to the ground.

"Gracie, we need to keep moving."

Two diseased stacked one on top of the other, and a third tried to force its way through. The first time three had tried to move through the same section of tunnel. Gracie shifted closer to them, waited for her moment, and stabbed it. Dead. There were now three stacked on top of one another.

Gracie waited, her own ragged breaths thrown back at

her in the tunnel. The next one couldn't get past the blockage. She pulled her legs up and curled into a ball. Turning back around, she crawled after William. Her throat dry, she talked with a croak, "By running and only killing one at a time, we were giving them space to get through. Now the tunnel's blocked, hopefully we can get out of here."

When Gracie had put about one hundred feet between her and the diseased, another wild scream lit up the tunnel. She spun around, and the strength left her body. Smothered by the depleting tug of fatigue, she sank onto the cold steel. "Shit!"

"Damn it," William said. "Let me have a go."

"You think you can do it better?"

"I think you need a rest."

Gracie nodded. "Thank you."

William turned around so he faced back down the tunnel.

Gracie slid past him, both of them on their sides, their fronts rubbing against one another. "Let's go back to back next time."

"Good idea." William picked up his sword from where she'd left it.

Gracie took her spear and led the way slowly down the tunnel, William sliding backwards after her.

Slap! Swish! Slap! Swish!

The tunnel's acoustics amplified the creature's deep death rattle.

Slap! Swish! Slap! Swish!

The skin on the back of Gracie's thighs tightened. Lit up with gooseflesh. But William had her back like she'd had his.

"Yeargh!" William's call ended in a wet squelch. A sword in a face. "Yeargh!" Another damp penetration.

Gracie halted, rolled onto her back, and watched. William had taken down two with two stabs. Her heart twisted when the third one came through. A child. Six or seven. It scooted over the corpses like a rat over a trash heap. Its once cherubic face now a gurning mask of hatred.

"Yeargh!"

Gracie closed her eyes, her shoulders snapping to her ears at the next crunch.

"Yeargh!" William spoke through panting breaths. "That's four of them. That should do for now."

"Let's swap over again so we can do this in shifts," Gracie said. "This might be slow going, but I think it's going to work."

CHAPTER 19

Thunk! Hawk connected the handle to the door and tugged. It popped open with a gentle *clack,* and the hinges groaned when he pulled the door wide.

Olga followed him into the armoury. Dark inside, she scrunched her nose, the cloying reek of metal and oil hanging heavy in the air. Although, she'd take this over the diseased stench any day. "How did you know the location of this place?"

"Aus and his crew came to this community to get ammo," Hawk said.

"I know that." Olga took a gun from Hawk. Like the guns she'd used in Dout, the heavy metal weapon had a good balance despite its poor aesthetic. She stood aside for Matilda to receive hers. "But you knew *exactly* where to come. You've not been inside this community before, have you?"

"I talked a lot with Moe."

"So that's where you were." Matilda held her arms so Hawk could load her with ammo. "I thought you might have been off somewhere with Dianna."

Hawk stacked another clump of magazines into her arms and stood up straight. He held eye contact with her, the light coming through the windows illuminating one side of his taut face.

"What?" Matilda shrugged. The magazines and gun knocked against one another in her arms. "We only knew she was an arsehole after we'd left Dout. You two were friends until that point."

"*Were* being the operative word." Hawk turned back to the ammo.

Olga found a couple of bags close by. Made from a thick brown hessian material, each had a zip along the top. She spread one open, and Matilda dropped in front of it. While Olga unloaded the magazines, she said, "We're certainly preparing for war, eh?"

Hawk hooked his foot around the second bag's handle and dragged it towards him. "Hope for the best ..." He filled the bag, several magazines at a time. "And the reason I hung out with Moe was because I couldn't be around anyone from our crew. I was resentful, and whenever I saw Artan, I took it out on him. I couldn't control it. I'm not proud of how I reacted. So the next best thing was to remove myself from the group whenever I could. Besides, I enjoyed being around Moe. He was a good guy." He zipped the bag closed. The magazines clinked together when he lifted it and threw it over his right shoulder. "Now let's get out of here."

Bagless, Olga loaded her gun and slapped the bottom of the magazine with a *clack!* She pointed the weapon out in front of her and led the way, poking her head from the armoury door. The community slept, and if there were guards about, they clearly had better things to do than be there.

Olga led them across the road and around the back of the communal building opposite. She waited for the other two to catch up. "Okay, so we have enough ammo to kill everyone in this place."

"I doubt it," Hawk said.

"Obviously." Olga rolled her eyes. "But hopefully this will help. However, we still have the same problem."

"We need to find Artan and Nick," Matilda said.

Olga's pulse spiked, and she pointed her gun at the hissing walkie-talkie clipped to Matilda's side.

Matilda freed the black device and pressed the button. "Don't you worry, peaches."

"What's with the peaches again?"

Hawk shrugged.

"When we get close to them, we'll know where they are. But first we need to get inside the community's walls."

Matilda turned the walkie-talkie off with a *click!*

"Shit, Matilda," Olga said, "I nearly shot you."

Her index finger on her right hand raised, Matilda silenced Olga.

Had anyone else done it, Olga would have snapped their finger off and shoved it up—

Clang! A struck bell, although not as clear. An industrial hammer against steel. A metal statue falling over.

"What is that?" Hawk said.

Matilda took off in the sound's direction.

Olga chased after her. While the external walls of this place were only twenty feet tall, the community dropped much lower inside. Were they on flat ground, many of the communal and industrial buildings would have stood taller than the steel perimeter. The entire community was shaped like a bowl. It allowed them to build higher and maintain their privacy. Even without a loaded bag, the incline they ran up sapped Olga's strength.

Behind Matilda and ahead of Hawk, Olga followed Matilda's lead. They ran along several small alleys between residential buildings, moving on tiptoes to keep the noise down. They ran deeper into the community towards the sound of the struck bell.

Matilda stopped, and Olga pulled up beside her, Hawk a few feet behind.

"What the hell is that thing?" Olga said. The external wall had a dog-leg bend, which had hidden it from sight. A pyramid with an illuminated transparent room on top. It stood just a few feet shorter than the external wall. It might not have been the tallest structure, but it didn't need to be with its elevated position in the community. Except for the wall, the glass room sat higher than everything else. Steel steps led up the pyramid's four sides. Several people congregated in the illuminated room.

"I don't know," Matilda said, "but I'm guessing that's where they're holding Artan and Nick."

Clang! It rang clearer than before.

"Yep." Matilda pointed. "They're up there."

Hawk unzipped his bag part way and slipped his hand inside. Easy access for when he wanted more ammo. "It's a good job we stopped at the armoury, then, eh?"

Olga tightened her grip on her gun. "It looks like we're about to go to war."

CHAPTER 20

"Argh!" Artan swung the chair against the steel wall separating his room and Nick's for a third time. *Clang!* The shock of the connection ran through its steel frame and made his hands buzz.

Five soldiers, the general, and their translator watched him. The soldiers from down the barrels of their guns.

The general shouted, his face turning redder than before.

The translator translated, "Do that once more and your friend dies!"

Artan tightened his grip on the steel chair and turned in the general's direction. Would this be his best chance to get out of there? His bonds lay coiled at his feet.

The general spoke in a calmer voice.

"Now," the translator said, "sit down and let one of my soldiers tie you up again. Any more nonsense from you and we'll make sure your friend's suffering is even worse. And you'll be made to watch."

As if on cue, Nick screamed from the other room. The sound ripped through Artan and turned the back of his knees weak.

The general smiled while he spoke.

"We can keep him in pain for days," the translator said. "We've had plenty of practice on people like you."

"You're people like me," Artan told the translator. "They might have adopted you as their pet, but don't forget who you are."

Wrinkles bunched at the edges of the translator's eyes. "While there may be truth in what you're saying, I'd be mad to pick the losing side, wouldn't I?"

Artan slumped in his chair. His walkie-talkie lay on the ground. Hopefully Matilda had heard him.

The general's shrill laugh bounced around the small room, his face now a beacon of mirth. Tears glistened in his black eyes. He pointed at Artan and laughed even harder. His soldiers laughed with him.

The translator translated, "It's only just occurred to me; you're in a room surrounded by glass, and you decide to attack the one wall that will never shatter. I almost feel sorry for you."

The general's humour vanished, and his jowls fell loose, pulling on the bottoms of his eyes.

The translator translated the single repeated word, "Almost."

Artan's swinging chair had gouged fresh scratches into the steel wall. They glistened in the bright light. A pathetic attempt at a breakout. No wonder the general found it funny.

The soldiers laughed even harder.

It might have been the middle of the night, but twenty to thirty people had climbed the stairs of the pyramid. Some gathered at the windows to Artan's side of the room. Many more headed for Nick's side. Nick screamed again, and several of the spectators applauded.

"It doesn't matter anyway," the translator said, relaying the general's message. "It's reinforced glass. Attack whatever wall you want; you're only getting out of here if *we* let you. But we're intrigued to meet your friends when they turn up. We have a welcoming committee at the gates."

"Please," Artan said to the general, "they've done nothing wrong."

The translator said, "They're trying to break into our community."

"Fuuuuuuuuuck!" Nick screamed again. Artan dropped his head. All this suffering because of him.

Crack!

A splash of red sprayed the glass wall. A spectator fell to their knees and slumped forward against the glass. Half of their face missing, they drew a streak of red down the other side of the transparent barrier.

Crack! Crack! Crack!

Two more fell.

The soldiers pointed their guns at the reinforced glass. For what good it did. They weren't laughing anymore. The spectators screamed and scattered. Matilda appeared a second later. She ran up the stairs while carrying a gun.

The general yelled. It didn't need to be translated. So much for his welcoming committee.

"Tilly!" Artan whispered.

The stuttered burst of bullet fire behind. Still strapped to his seat, a twinge ran up Artan's back when he twisted to see Olga run across the outside of the room towards the door. She screamed, kicked her way into the room, and opened fire. Hawk charged in after her.

The five soldiers didn't have time to turn around before she and Hawk mowed them all down. While Olga ran for Nick's room, Hawk shot the general in the face, a red puff of mist bursting from the back of his head. As the fat man fell, he raised his gun at the translator.

"Hawk, no!" Artan yelled.

Hawk tilted his head to one side. "No?"

"He's just the translator. He's one of us. Don't shoot him."

An already pale man, the translator turned damn near translucent. He trembled in the face of Hawk's aggression and yelped, flinching away from the spray of concrete when Hawk shot into the ground in front of him.

Hawk's bullets broke the translator's chain. "That's the best we can do for now." He pointed his gun at him again. "Unless you want me to try to shoot your necklace off you too?"

"No!" the translator said. "And t-thank you." He pulled up the excess chain. "I-if you don't mind, I can take the key from the general and remove the lock?"

"Where is it?" Hawk said.

The translator still shook when he pointed down at the terracotta man. "It's amongst those keys on his belt."

Hawk kept his gun fixed on the translator and crouched down. He pulled hard to rip the man's buckle, dragging the fat general across the ground a few feet before the jangling ring of keys tore loose. He threw them at the translator.

"Artan!" Matilda ran into the room and slammed the door shut behind her. She came to his side and undid his ropes. "You're okay!"

"Thank you!" Artan pushed away from his chair and ran into the room after Olga. The two soldiers who'd accompanied the torturer lay dead on the floor. Olga held the tall woman at gunpoint. She'd forced her to kneel. She'd also untied Nick, who sat slumped in his chair, covered in his own blood, deep gashes on his chest and arms.

"Nick!" Artan ran to him. "Nick, are you okay?"

Nick's eyes rolled, but he forced a delirious smile. "You should have seen the other person."

Tears blurred Artan's vision. He tore the shirt from one of the dead soldiers and ripped it into strips. He wrapped

Nick's arms first. The cuts were so deep his body looked like chopped liver. Blood seeped through the fabric faster than Artan could dress his wounds. The tighter he tied them, the more Nick bled. "I'm so sorry. I screwed up. And I punished you when I thought you'd landed us in here. But this was all my fault. I'm so sorry."

Tearing more strips free, Artan wrapped them around Nick's chest. "We'll get you cleaned up when we get out of here. Can you walk?"

"Yeah." Nick nodded. "I think so. And please don't feel bad, Artan. It's not your fault."

If only Artan had even a shred of Nick's grace.

Matilda stood in the doorway, and Olga remained over the torturer, her gun aimed at her head.

"Give that to me." Artan took Olga's gun. He shouted, "Look at me!" His voice bounced off the hard walls. Some spectators remained outside the room. Artan shot a spray of bullets at the reinforced glass, and they scattered like spooked pigeons.

"Get the translator in here," Artan said.

The pale man entered, a red hoop of a rash around his neck from where he'd worn the chains.

"Tell her to look at me," Artan said.

The man translated, and the torturer looked up. Maybe he should have taken more time to make her suffer, but when one half of her mouth lifted in a smile, Artan yelled and squeezed the trigger. The gun bucked in his hands, and the bullets ripped her smug face to shreds.

Out of ammo and the torturer down, but Artan continued to squeeze the trigger and point the gun at her. Her limp and bleeding form blurred through his tears.

"Give it to me." Olga took her gun back. "We need to get moving. We might all be together, and we might all be armed, but we're nowhere near safe. We still have a lot to do before we're away from here. We had stealth on our side when we came in. We definitely won't have it on the way out."

While the spectators went one way, running down the pyramid's stairs, soldiers came the other, charging up. They closed in on them from all four sides. At least fifty men and women in the green uniform of their army, they were all armed.

Artan took the guns from both the soldiers Olga had killed. He handed one to the translator. "You with us?"

The translator's throat bobbed with his gulp. He peered out of the windows at those closing in. His eyes narrowed, and he rubbed his neck. "Yeah, I'm with you."

"Right, let's get out of here, then."

CHAPTER 21

Gracie shoved open the hatch at the end of the tunnel and inhaled. She threw her spear out ahead of her and crawled after it, dragging herself along the ground on her front. Her water bladders remained full at her sides, as they'd been all the way down the tunnel. Her elbows throbbed from where she'd slammed them down against the steel again and again in her desperation to be born back into the world once more. To leave behind the foetid womb that had once been her home. To start anew, rings or not.

The same cloudy night sky they'd left behind when they went into Dout. No matter how long she'd lived there, when she'd been in the bowels of her home, she'd never been able to keep track of time in the outside world. The position of the moon had shifted. A few hours had passed. A few wasted hours. What had she achieved by coming here? Other than nearly getting her and William killed. They would have been better off waiting in the cottage and resting in preparation for climbing the wall. But what if she hadn't gone back? Would she always have wondered about the rings? At least she'd tried. She could now accept they were lost.

On her feet, Gracie pulled William's sword away and tossed it aside, grabbed both of his hands, and walked backwards, dragging him out on his stomach. The tunnel was darker than the evening. Impossible to tell how close the diseased were to clearing the latest blockage they'd left in their path. Hopefully they had enough time to get out of there.

Gracie closed the hatch gently. They seemed alone, but you could never tell. Sometimes the diseased materialised from thin air. The camouflage on top of the hatch made it one with its surroundings.

A tacky layer of dried sweat clung to Gracie's skin. She wiped her brow with the back of her sleeve, and her eyes were sticky when she blinked. Who knew when she'd get a chance to shower again. But at least they were free of the thick funk of the diseased. Of their own sweaty struggle to get away from them.

Crack!

The steel hatch opened and slammed shut again.

Gracie sighed and raised her eyebrows at William.

He shrugged. "They were going to get through eventually. They did every other time."

"It would have been nice if it had taken them a little longer though," Gracie said.

Crack!

The steel hatch opened and slammed shut again.

"Come on." Gracie tugged William's arm before turning from him and walking away. "Let's get out of here."

Instead of following her, William ran to the pile of diseased Max had slain. Evidence of his final protective act. One of many. Evidence of the burden placed upon him by the rest of the group. The slayer of diseased. A one-man industry. He'd bailed them out time and time again.

William lifted a diseased's ankles and dragged them from the pile.

"What are you doing?" Gracie said.

The woman's arms, as limp as the rest of her, stretched out behind her and ploughed a line through the damp grass. Two diseased rolled from the pile where William had unsettled the structure's integrity. He dragged the woman across the hatch. "I'm blocking the tunnel. Stopping them coming out."

Crack!

The tunnel's hatch lifted and dropped again. The weight of one bloated corpse made a difference, but nowhere near enough.

"They haven't worked out how to exit the tunnel. When they finally do, I want to make sure they can't." William jogged back to the mound of cadavers. "Send the diseased back into Dout rather than after us. Make it hard for those who would do us harm to—"

"Do us harm?" Grace said.

"Right." William ran backwards, dragging another diseased with him. He laid it across the first and returned to the pile for a third time.

Crack!

The tunnel's hatch lifted and dropped again. Lower than before.

Gracie joined William, averting her eyes when she passed her brother's corpse. She didn't need the reminder. She'd taken his mum, his home, and his life. No matter how she justified it, no matter how much of an arsehole he'd been, it didn't undo her actions. She grabbed a diseased by its ankles and dragged it to the hatch.

~

Ten to fifteen bodies covered the hatch. They crisscrossed one another, each one adding their weight to the pile keeping the tunnel closed.

Crack!

Muted through the rotten cadavers. The hatch remained closed. "We done?" Gracie said.

William added another corpse to the pile. The moonlight caught the dark sheen of his sweating skin. He stepped back from the mound, hands on his hips. He nodded. "Yeah, we're done." He walked away.

"So what are you doing now?" Gracie said.

William continued towards Aus' body.

Gracie's heart raced. "Leave him there. He doesn't go on the pile."

But William ignored her.

"I mean it, William. Leave him!" If she'd known how Aus felt, they might have been able to reconcile their differences. But he hadn't given her a chance. He'd made her kill him. No, he hadn't. She'd killed him, and she'd meant it. She couldn't blame him for that. But he'd killed Max, and he'd made her life hell from the second she'd been born. "William!"

Like he hadn't heard her, William crouched down next to Aus. His head tilted to one side. He pitied what Gracie had done to him. And he should. She'd taken his mum. She'd taken his home. She'd taken his life. Everything would have been better for him were she not there. Gracie said, "Stop!"

But William reached down to Aus' face. He laid a hand along his cheek. "You did nothing wrong."

"Are you taking Aus' side?" Gracie said.

"No." William shook his head. "I'm talking to you, Gracie. Like I've already said, you did nothing wrong. Max made the choice to go outside Dout, not you. If you were certain someone had seen him, you would have acted. It would have been the right thing to do. But you didn't know what was coming. How could you? So you protected your friends. And you had no control over how your mum treated you, and how Aus reacted to that. You were a baby. It wasn't your fault."

The world blurred through her tears. Gracie bit on her quivering bottom lip. The lump in her throat strangled her response.

"I believe that those looking down on us don't do so in judgement, but with love and understanding. No matter what, they see you're doing your best. We all are." William reached around the back of Aus' neck.

Gracie rubbed her sore eyes to help her see them better. The moon drew a thin highlight along them. They hung from William's grip. A thin silver chain, two rings at the bottom.

"Are these what you were looking for?" William said.

Gracie ran over to her brother's body, but William met her halfway. He reached around and tied the silver chain at the back of her neck. She threw her arms around him and squeezed. "Thank you. Thank you so much. Motherfucker!"

"Huh?" William stepped back.

"Aus," Gracie said. "He told me to stay out of Dad's room when we were leaving. He spoke like me going in there would be disrespectful. He made me feel bad for even considering it. He made *me* feel like the arsehole, but he'd already looted the place. What a snake." She held the rings in her fist in front of her chest. "We were destined to never get on. I can see that now. As the oldest, he decided he hated me before he'd given me a chance. What could I do?"

"Exactly. You tried. And had he tried to reach out to you, you would have worked through it with him."

Tears blurred her vision again. Gracie nodded and sniffed against her running nose. "I would have. I so wanted a big brother in my life. I hated him, but I love him."

William looked at the sky. "I think he can see that now."

Gracie tucked the rings into her shirt. They rested against her chest. The pressure of a reassuring hand. They had her back. They'd be watching over her. They'd help her navigate what lay ahead.

Crack!

Futile attempts to be let out of the tunnel. The diseased beat against it again.

"I'm sorry I dragged you back into Dout," she said. "If only we'd known the rings were out here all along."

William smiled. "At least we've found them. That's the main thing."

Pressing a hand to her chest, Gracie nodded. "Thank you. Now let's get back to the cottage and see how the others got on."

CHAPTER 22

"You sure we can trust him with a gun?" Olga pointed at the skinny translator with her own.

"Yeah," Artan said. "He worked for them, but he isn't one of them. He had no choice."

The translator stared at the ground while they spoke. A naughty child awaiting the punishment of their parents.

Nick filled the doorway in the steel wall between the two rooms. He leaned against the frame for support. How the hell were they supposed to get out with him in tow? But they had to try. Max had died because Olga had failed him. She couldn't let the same happen to Nick. Whatever it took, they'd walk away from this. Even if she had to sacrifice herself to make it happen.

Green-uniformed soldiers swarmed the stairs leading up all four sides of the pyramid. They only had one door leading in and out of the room. Olga passed Nick and ran to it, the bulletproof glass her shield. She leaned against it, close to the door. Hawk joined her.

There were about fifteen to twenty soldiers on each side of the pyramid. Several of them fired warning shots against the glass. The vibrations of the impact shook through Olga, and the bullets left black scuff-marks against the transparent barrier.

An almost full magazine, Olga continued to use the glass wall as a shield, opened the door, and poked her gun out. She held the heavy weapon with one hand and pulled the trigger. The recoil gave it a life of its own. She shot the sky and the ground twice as many times as she shot in the soldiers' direction, but she finally caught one. A young teenager dressed in a uniform that didn't fit, his left arm snapped away from his body, he dropped his gun, and he fell sideways down the steel pyramid's steps.

Olga pulled back into the safety of the room. "They're just kids."

"Kids who are trying to kill us," Hawk said. "We have to fight back. We've got to take down another sixty to eighty of the bastards."

Olga nodded. Hawk had a point. She ripped the empty magazine free and discarded it on the concrete floor. Hawk passed her a new one, which she slotted in, slapping the bottom so it connected with a *crack!* She pointed the gun outside the room and shot again.

"I think I know why they've sent kids," Artan said. He stood close to Nick and the translator, his gun raised, his eyes wild. "We saw a whole load of soldiers on their way to Dout. We think they were going there to take control of it tonight. They must have left the reserves behind to defend the place."

"Shit!" Olga pointed her gun from the door.

"That isn't a good thing?" Artan shared a glance with Nick. "I assumed that would make our lives easier."

Matilda stood on the other side of the room, tracking the soldiers approaching them. She shouted across, "That's where William and Gracie have gone."

"They're not at the cottage?" Artan said.

The clatter of Olga's firing gun made her ears ring.

Matilda waited for her to pull back in and reload before she spoke again. "Gracie needed to get some bits before we crossed the wall."

"When did you see them?" Olga said. *Crack!* She fitted the magazine.

"When we were on the wall testing the magnets. Around the time we spoke to you on the walkie-talkie."

"And you didn't think to tell us?"

"It didn't seem relevant."

"It was relevant." Olga leaned against the wall for support. She unloaded her next magazine on the soldiers. The kids. She must have sent over one hundred bullets down on them, and she'd only hit one damn soldier. And even then, she'd only clipped him.

The soldiers on Olga's side made it to the top and leaned against the glass. Separated by a matter of feet and the transparent barrier, their proximity revealed the reality of just how young they were. Some of them were barely teenagers. But they were armed. They intended to kill her if she didn't kill them. More soldiers reached the top of the pyramid on the other sides.

The steel partition bisecting the room blocked Olga's view of the glass wall on the left. But if the soldiers had reached the other three sides, they must have reached the fourth by now too.

"Eighteen," Hawk said. He nodded at the glass. "There's eighteen of them on this side."

"That's probably their combined age too," Olga said.

Artan pointed at a soldier close to Matilda's side of the room. "What's that?" The girl wore a uniform several sizes too big. She held a spherical metal object. She removed a pin from it and held aloft before tossing it in through the open roof.

"Throw it back!" Nick said.

The translator had already charged towards it. He picked up the palm-sized sphere and launched it back out again. The soldiers scattered.

Whomp! The bright explosion dazzled Olga. The shock of the detonation shook the ground. Black scorch marks painted the other side of the transparent wall.

Nick hugged himself as if he could somehow hold all his cuts together, his face a constantly shifting sequence of grimaces. Olga nodded at him and then at the translator. "Thank you."

Chink!

Another one landed in the room.

Artan grabbed it and threw it back. It exploded in the air above them, the heat shoving Olga against the wall.

"They're holding onto them for longer," Hawk said. "Soon they're going to time it right, and one will explode before we can send it back. We need to get out of here."

Olga stood by the only exit. They were fighting scared kids. Kids who'd probably never seen battle before. That gave them the advantage. "Yeargh!" She burst from the room, the stock of her gun nestled in her shoulder. She aimed at the line of soldiers pressed against the other side of the glass. The one at the front held a spherical explosive. She unloaded several bullets into his chest. He twitched, spasmed, and fell sideways, rolling down the steel steps of the pyramid.

Olga ducked back in to avoid the return fire. The soldier rolling down the stairs exploded, his corpse losing an arm and half his face.

The momentary distraction gave Olga her opening. She stepped out of the room again and fired on the soldiers.

Where they lined up, only one of them could fight at any one time. The poor bastards queued up to be executed.

Olga pulled back in and loaded her next magazine. *Crack!* She remained in the room this time and hung her gun from the door again. She took down the first soldier before she stepped out, improved her aim with the stability of a wider stance, and unloaded on those behind. Her cheeks shook with the kicking gun. The soldiers peeled away one after the next, rolling down the pyramid like those before them.

A bullet hit the glass a foot behind Olga's head. Hawk stepped from the room and shot the already wounded soldier lying across the stairs. She should have seen him.

Eighteen soldiers, at least ten of them were down. The rest had pulled around the side of the illuminated room to join the others. The clear walls highlighted their utter disorganisation. They had no leaders.

Olga remained outside, Hawk with her. They'd won this advantage. They weren't giving it up. She reached into Hawk's bag, took another magazine, and reloaded her gun.

Another explosive came over from Matilda's side of the room. It landed, rolled along the floor, and continued out through the door and down the stairs. Olga and Hawk pulled away, turning their back on the explosion's ball of heat.

Her ears ringing, Olga poked her head back in the room and shouted at the others, "We need to get moving now!"

The translator held his gun and ran from the room first, Matilda a few steps behind him. Artan supported Nick's weight and helped him out after them.

"We need to clear the pyramid," Olga said. "These kids don't know what they're doing, so I say we go fully offensive."

Matilda nodded and pulled the translator with her when she ran away from Olga and Hawk. They'd go around one side of the square room each. They might have been outnumbered, but the soldiers who'd used the wall as cover were now exposed. How long before they retreated behind the opposite wall?

Like she'd done to get out of the room, Olga leaned around the next corner and shot. She had cover, and the soldiers on that side seemed yet to realise they didn't. Maybe they were under strict orders to stand and fight. They fell away from the glass wall, tumbling and rolling down the stairs towards the ground. This time, Olga scanned the fallen, sending a few extra bullets into the still-writhing forms.

Most of the soldiers down, the final few retreated around the last wall and fired behind them as they ran. For what good it did. Olga had pulled back into cover. She took another magazine from Hawk's bag while he took her place, shooting at the few still-exposed kids. They died for the city because they were too young to do anything but follow orders.

Her arms buzzing and her fingers sore from holding the vibrating gun, Olga took a little longer changing the magazine.

Artan exited the room, supporting Nick's weight. He led them towards Matilda and the translator, who were dispatching the soldiers on their side.

The steel wall bisecting the illuminated room blocked Olga's line of sight. Matilda and the translator vanished behind it, pressing their advantage. A few seconds later, Olga took Hawk around their side.

Blood and bodies coated the stairs. Another one of the fallen rolled onto their side, and Olga sent a spray of bullets into the top of her head. Her skull turned to red mist, and her flaccid body slid a few feet farther down.

A crowd of people gathered at the bottom. But they didn't wear uniforms, and they weren't carrying guns. Olga wagged a finger at Hawk. They weren't at war with civilians. Bad enough they had to fight children.

Instead of defending their position, the remaining soldiers retreated and stood together in the middle of the last wall as a pack, waiting to be shot. Olga obliged. Fifteen to twenty soldiers, some tried to defend their position. They fell first. The remaining soldiers ran, which made life much easier. No crossfire between her side and Matilda's. They picked them off, shooting them in the back as they retreated.

The spray of bullets animated every soldier as they fell. Their limp bodies slammed against the hard stairs. Their momentum carried them most of the way to the ground. With no one left to defend them, the spectators vanished.

Most of the city stretched away from Olga and the others, the dog-leg bend in the wall on their right. The dog pen and the tunnel out of there around that corner. Three to four thousand small houses between them and freedom. The spectators had retreated for now, but, in the clear absence of their usual army, what if they took matters into their own hands and defended their homes? They needed to be gone before the civilians' fear turned into aggression.

The entire pyramid clear for now, Matilda and the translator emerged from their side as Olga and Hawk stepped out. Olga made the hand gesture for okay to Matilda, who returned it. They were clear. Artan came around the corner last, straining under Nick's weight.

Olga called across to Matilda, "You ready to go?"

Matilda pointed down to her left, away from her and Olga. "Yes. And we need to be quick about it."

Green-uniformed soldiers swarmed through the residential buildings below. Probably more rookies, but they had the numerical advantage, and they were closing in fast.

Pointing down the pyramid on her side, Olga said, "This way. Now!"

CHAPTER 23

Artan's gun hung down across his front from its leather strap. It swung against his stomach from where he had a hold of Nick instead of his weapon. He supported Nick's weight on one side, and the translator supported Nick from the other. Nick's head hung limp, and his feet dragged along the ground. He muttered things Artan couldn't understand and didn't have the time to decipher. They needed to get out of there.

The steel wall on their right, they'd left the pyramid well behind them. They passed around the dog-leg bend and weaved through the small houses on their way to the back wall and the tunnel.

The translator looked behind and stumbled. The army on their tail screamed as they charged.

"Will you focus on what you're doing?" Artan said.

"It's kinda tricky with that lot behind us."

"There's nothing we can do. Let the others take care of them."

Olga and Hawk ran ahead, Matilda behind. They had

enough ammo to fight an army, but they had nowhere near enough people or guns. They had to be smart about this.

Leading the way, Olga took them left around the side of what looked like a warehouse. A larger building than the surrounding houses. At least fifteen feet tall, each wall of the square structure stretched thirty feet wide.

Before Artan and the translator followed, Olga came back and shooed them away. "There are more soldiers that way."

"Shit!" the translator said. "This won't end well if we get caught."

"Then we won't get caught," Artan said.

They jogged back into the mazy paths snaking through the small houses.

"How many translators do they have in this place?" Artan said.

"You're asking me that now?"

Although out of breath, Artan shrugged. "We're moving as fast as we can." They could hardly sprint while carrying Nick.

"I dunno," the translator said. "A handful at any one time."

"So if they can understand what we're saying, why didn't they try to talk to the people of Dout?"

"Dout?"

"The underground community they went to war with."

The translator's pale and gaunt face glistened with sweat. "They don't care what you have to say unless what you have to say is information that will help them eradicate you. They hate you. They only used us to take on patrol with them on the off chance we'd catch something of what you're saying and give them information that would help their goal. The— oh shit!"

Olga had stopped again.

A row of small houses on either side of them. Butted against one another, they created a long alley. Soldiers blocked the way ahead. The group behind continued to close in. Their only escape would be over the roofs. But Nick didn't have climbing in him.

Matilda kept her gun levelled on the army behind them and backed towards Artan. Olga and Hawk did the same.

"We're trapped," the translator said. His breathing grew ragged, his eyes wide as he looked from one end of the alley to the other. "And they won't kill us here. That would be too easy." He clapped his hands to the sides of his face. "I knew I shouldn't have come with you."

"You panicking isn't helping," Artan said. He flicked his head towards the house closest to them, and the translator helped him rest Nick down, so he sat leaning against the wall. Two small children peered out of the window and then ducked when Artan looked at them.

"I can't take any more of this place," the translator said. "I won't let them catch me again."

"What ar—"

The translator shoved his gun's barrel into his mouth and pulled the trigger. A spray of red burst towards the sky. He snapped rigid and fell forwards. Blood and brain matter leaked from the hole in the top of his head.

"Shit!" Nick watched on, wide-eyed.

"How are you doing?" Artan said.

"Better than him." Nick shook his head.

Matilda fired a burst at the army behind them. Olga and Hawk did the same with those in front. Warning shots. They kept them pinned back.

"Tilly, how long can you hold them back for?"

"Until I need to reload."

"Olga?"

"The same. We need to think of a way out of here, and fast."

"I'm only doing this because I have to," Artan said to Nick.

"Wha—"

Artan slammed the butt of his gun against the window the kids had stared from. It broke with a loud *crash*, driving all the glass into the house. The kids inside screamed. A man and woman shouted.

Artan ran his gun around the inside of the frame to clear out the glass shards and climbed into the house. His throat dry, his stomach clamped. Footsteps ran away from him up the stairs, but before he followed them, he checked the kitchen. Empty. He climbed the stairs one at a time, his gun pointed out in front of him.

The door to the bedroom on the left hung open. A family of four huddled together on the double bed. The kids were about three and five years old. The girl, the youngest. Artan fought his own weakening voice when he shouted at the parents, "Let go of them. Now!"

Both the man and the woman cried and shook their heads. At that moment, they spoke the same language.

"Now!" Artan walked closer, his gun raised higher. He'd blow their fucking brains out if they pushed him. He tugged the little girl's twig-thin arm. Her dad clung to her other hand.

Artan slammed the butt of his gun across the side of the man's face. It connected with a wet *clop* and threw the man to the floor. Artan pulled the wailing girl free and shoved her towards the door.

His gun aimed at the parents, Artan fought to speak through his own wavering voice. "Let go!"

The parents' faces hung slack with horror.

What kind of monster did this to a family? The kind of monster who hid in children's rooms while they were sleeping. The kind of monster who blamed the people he cared about for their mistakes. The kind of monster who had it in him to place the lives of him and his friends over the well-being of a kid.

He dragged the boy free, the mum giving up her son more easily than the dad had his daughter. A small holdall on the floor, Artan took it and threw some of the man's clothes inside. Nick would need them when they were free of this place.

Pointing down the stairs with his gun, Artan showed the kids where to go. Their small shoulders bobbed, and they hung their heads as they followed his direction. Flat-footed steps, their small bare feet hit the steel as they trudged away from their mummy and daddy. If only the translator hadn't blown his brains out. He could have promised the little ones they'd be okay.

Artan kicked the front door wide and shoved the children out first. He pushed them in Olga's direction.

"What the hell are you doing?"

"We need hostages," Artan said.

"They're kids."

"We're not going to hurt them. But we need them to think we will so the army will let us go."

A magnetic handle on the inside of the door, Artan twisted it clear, crossed to the neighbouring house, and entered their home next.

∾

When Artan emerged with two more children, another girl and boy, Olga sneered.

"I'm all ears if you have a better way of getting us out of here?"

Olga shook her head.

The four children in front of them, Artan and Olga forced

them into the army's line of sight, and Artan shouted, "Do you have a translator with you?"

"Yes." A woman with a chain around her neck stumbled into the alley, shoved from behind.

"The only way these kids will survive is if you let us walk out of here unharmed."

The translator spoke to someone in the army, and a man replied, their voice raised. They shouted across to their comrades at the other end of the alley.

"Okay," the translator said. "We'll escort you out to make sure you don't do them any harm. If you so much as lay a finger on them, all bets are off."

Artan nodded at Olga. "But you only need a small group of you to escort us. Four at the most. Four and you."

The translator relayed the message and said, "Okay. Fine."

Artan would never feel proud of what he'd done to these poor kids, but so far it had worked. And better he lived with the guilt than they all died at the hands of these sadistic bastards.

CHAPTER 24

Artan shoved the crying kids towards Hawk when they reached the supply hut near the kennels. They'd cried all the way, dragging their feet, their small forms hunched. He pushed one of the little girls a bit too hard and winced when she stumbled on the edge of her balance, her thin arms windmilling as she fought to remain upright. Bad enough he'd taken them from their homes in the middle of the night. He didn't need to be shoving them over too. But they had to get out of this place. If they let the people of this community capture them, they'd never leave. What they'd done to Nick would seem tame by comparison. "Keep an eye on these, will you?"

Hawk stepped back from the kids. And who could blame him for wanting nothing to do with them? With what Artan had done.

"Look," Artan said, "I'm not happy about it either." He spoke with a raised voice so the others heard. "But no one else offered any better ideas. If we can get out of this place and away without causing these kids any harm, I'd say it was a good choice."

The translator and four soldiers remained close by, watching on. They'd followed at a respectable distance. They were here to chaperone the children and nothing more. The soldiers listened to the translator's interpretations of Artan's words.

Hawk accepted what had to be done with a slight incline of his head.

Artan propped Nick up against the wall of the small supply hut. He leaned close and waited for Nick to focus on him. "I'm going to leave you here for a moment. Is that okay?"

His voice weak, his words slurred, Nick said, "Just get on with it." He slid down the wall, hit the ground with a jolt, and dragged air in through his clenched teeth.

"Are you—"

"Just hurry, Artan!"

Artan jumped and kicked the side of the hut, boosting himself off the wall. He caught the roof's right-angled edge. His boots slipped as he struggled for purchase, his soles wet with dew.

The two bags were where he'd left them. Artan tugged one free and tossed it down. It landed in front of Olga with a *crash!* She lifted the heavy bag, grunting with the effort. He dropped the next one for Matilda. Between the magnets in the bags and the ones outside the community, they had forty-four in total. Hopefully, it would be enough. It had to be. No chance they were coming back again.

Being higher than everyone else and most of the short buildings in the community gave Artan a better view of the place. Of the army heading for the front gates. They might have agreed to let them move on with the kids, but no way would they let them leave with them. Two hundred strong, it would take a miracle to get past them. Were they heading that way. They clearly knew nothing about the tunnel behind the kennel.

Artan hung down from the roof of the hut and dropped the final few feet. He bent his knees to soften his landing. Better the others didn't know about the army. What purpose would it serve? They didn't need the added pressure, and it changed nothing. They had to get away from there. And fast. He pointed his gun at the children. All four of them screamed and cried. The soldiers shouted at him.

"Tell them I won't hurt the kids," Artan said.

The translator spoke to the soldiers. "Then what are you doing?"

"Giving my friends time to get out of here. This will only turn sour if you attack us."

The translator relayed the message to the soldiers. They offered no reply.

"You ready for this?" Artan said.

His friends nodded.

"We need to be quick and efficient."

Olga turned to Nick. "Do you have that in you?"

Despite grimacing every few seconds, sweat glistening on his brow, and him breathing with his entire body, Nick tutted.

Olga shrugged and led the way across the small ledge along the back of the dog pen. At least fifty dogs beneath her. They barked and jumped up at the wall. But none of them could jump high enough. She trembled from where she held the bag of magnets away from her, keeping them as far from any metal surface as possible.

The soldiers and the translator talked amongst themselves, their words quick, their voices raised. They pointed at Olga. They'd clearly never seen this exit before.

Just before Matilda followed her, Artan grabbed her arm. She carried a bag of ammo in one hand and a bag of magnets in the other. He would have helped her, but he needed his hands free to hold the gun, and he already carried a bag of clean clothes for Nick. "Make sure you lie over the bag when you crawl through the tunnel. Tell Olga to do the same. It will keep it from attaching to the surrounding walls."

Matilda glanced at the waiting soldiers and the four distraught children. "Be careful, okay? Make sure they don't misread your intentions." She followed Olga.

"Now," Hawk said to Nick as he helped him to the ledge. "Lean back into the wall. I don't fancy falling into that pen."

For Nick's entire crossing, Artan divided his attention between him, the kids, and the soldiers. His heart beat in his throat. If Nick fell, he'd be screwed. No fighting his way out this time.

But Nick made it across and slipped into the space between the back of the kennel and the wall.

His gun still levelled on the children, Artan called across to the translator, "I need you to repeat this to the kids."

The translator's chain rattled when she nodded. But the four soldiers spoke to her, and she said, "Where are you going?"

As far away from that mob at the front gates as possible. "You don't need to worry about our destination," Artan said. "All that matters is we're going away from here, never to return. Now tell the kids this." While he spoke, Artan walked backwards across the narrow ledge. One step at a time. His throat hurt from shouting over the snarling and barking dogs below. "First, children, you need to stay exactly where you are. If you don't, I will shoot you."

The wall was damp with the early morning dew. The kids cried harder than before as the translator relayed Artan's instructions to them.

"I'm sorry," Artan said, pausing long enough to let the translator finish. "You don't deserve what's happening to you. It's a stressful thing to go through. But my friends and I are scared too. We're scared that we might get killed in this place, so we took you with us because we knew they would leave us alone if we did that."

After a pause to let the narrator catch up, Artan reached the tight space between the back of the kennel and the wall. "I just want you to know how incredibly sorry I am for taking you. I never meant you any harm. The only reason I took you was because you were in the houses closest to me. This community is powerful and well protected. You're safe here. I won't be back, and they'll make sure this can't ever happen to you again. You're going to be okay."

One soldier yelled, whipped their gun up, and shot at Artan. The bullet hit the side of the kennel with a loud *ting!* Artan ducked into the space between the kennel and the wall, avoiding the soldier's next assault. The others joined the first, and bullets pinged off the steel walls surrounding him.

Artan's panic echoed when he dragged his upper body into the tight tunnel. A bullet whipped across the back of his calf, batting the fabric of his trousers. An inch lower and it would have torn a hole in his leg.

Out of the other side, Olga pulled Artan free and said, "We need to get moving."

They did. They had an army descending on them. Sweat dampened Nick's brow. Just standing still pushed him to his limit. It would be slow going with him and the magnets. Artan took Matilda's bag of ammo. "Hawk, come with me."

At a small mound nearby, Artan emptied out Matilda's magazines and threw down the bag of clean clothes he'd taken for Nick.

"What are you doing?" Hawk said.

Artan took Hawk's bag of ammo and did the same. A mound of metal. "We came here for the magnets. We need these bags to ensure we leave with them." He tossed one of the empty bags at Hawk. "Come on."

The pair of them returned to the back wall. The army would have gotten the message by now. They'd be on their way. But what good would it do to tell the others? Nick didn't need the pressure, and it wasn't like they didn't all have the same desire to get away from there as fast as they could.

Artan threw his bag down and filled it with half the magnets he and Nick had picked up on their first trip into the community. He slipped his and Nick's spear sheaths on his back. When the bullets ran out, they needed something. Hawk mirrored his actions.

His bag full, Artan moved to the tunnel, shoved the bush aside, poked the end of his gun in, and pulled the trigger. The soldier inside screamed until they didn't. Of course they'd followed them. They would have been killed by their own if they hadn't.

A temporary fix. They might have deterred the four soldiers, but the army was coming.

Back on the brow of the hill, Artan said, "I'm going to wait here and hold them back. It'll give you time to get away. I'll catch up."

Nick grabbed him, his voice weak. "Come with us now."

"You need the time. I can give you that."

Nick's face twisted. Something deeper than the physical pain from his lacerations. "Promise me you'll get back to the cottage."

"It's only four soldiers and a translator," Artan said. The warble in his voice almost betrayed him. Four soldiers, a translator, and a two-hundred-strong army hell-bent on their destruction and torture. They might have only been kids, but when the numbers were stacked so heavily in their favour ...

"Promise me."

Artan kissed him and then pushed him away. "I will. Now go."

Olga, Matilda, and Hawk all carried a bag of magnets. Artan kept one with him. Hawk took Nick's weight like Artan had.

Nick said, "You're sure you want to do this?"

"Yes."

Matilda held back, but Artan shooed her away. "I've got this. See you at the cottage."

Her brow pinched in the middle.

"Go. Please."

Matilda pointed at him. "You'd best come back." She ran after the others.

About fifty feet from the back wall, Artan lay on the damp ground on his front, behind the small mound. An enormous pile of ammo beside him. Would this plan work, or would it be his last stand? How had the translator done it? Barrel in the mouth and point up. If it came to it, anything had to be better than getting captured by the army. And his life would be a small price to pay if it guaranteed the others' safety.

CHAPTER 25

He owed them this. All of them. Nick had been tortured because Artan screwed up. Matilda, well, the list stretched on forever: His sister, his saviour, his best friend. Hawk and Olga would do the same for him. Hell, they had. They'd run into this community and put their lives on the line to get him and Nick out of the situation he'd caused. But he could make everything better now. His plan would work, even if the butterflies in his stomach begged to differ. His friends would have been as doubtful if he'd told them. But he needed them to leave, so he kept it to himself.

The steel wall stretched both ways, the dog-leg bend to Artan's left, a corner of the community about one hundred feet to his right. He twisted on the damp ground, his clothes soaked from the dew on the grass. Closing one eye, he peered down the barrel of his ugly gun and shot right at the corner edge of the community. His gun shook, and the bullets that hit made the steel sing. Many shot past.

The bush by the tunnel shifted. Artan turned his attention on it just as his magazine ran out of ammo. "Shit!" He pulled it out, tossed it aside, and reloaded.

The soldier stood up from the tunnel, and Artan shot him, pinning him to the wall. The soldier's body snapped and twitched before he slumped to the ground. "Two down. Two to go." Hopefully the translator would have the good sense to stay out of it and remain inside the community. He had no beef with her.

His aim on the corner again, Artan unloaded several more magazines, tossing each one aside when they emptied. His hands buzzed, his gun grew hotter, and his ears rang.

An explosion of mud burst just a few feet in front of Artan, spraying him with dirt. The next soldier from the tunnel had their gun pointed at him.

Artan unloaded the rest of his magazine into him.

A fresh magazine in his gun, his focus back on the corner of the wall, Artan sent another wave of bullets into it. But he kept half an eye on the tunnel's exit. He wouldn't get caught unawares again. He loaded the next magazine, fired until it emptied, and then loaded the next.

∾

Artan dispatched the last of the four soldiers to crawl through the tunnel. He shot the rustling bush, and it stopped rustling. They should have stayed inside the community and kept their lives. Although, if they returned without fighting, would their punishment be worse than anything he did to them?

About ten magazines remained beside him. Artan discarded another empty and reloaded. A continuous, high-pitched tone rang in his ears. It drilled into his brain. But it didn't mask the thunderous footsteps closing in on his position. The army was on their way, and they were close. His plan had failed.

"Shit!" Artan said. He slammed a fist into the ground. "Shit!"

Artan got to his feet. His last stand. If he gave the others time to get away, then he'd done a good thing, right? He'd save a magazine for himself. Bottom of the barrel against the underside of his chin. No way would he let them take him back inside.

A shrill cry on his right. It came from the meadow. The moon shone on the long grass. On the clumsy army closing in. At least one hundred diseased. Enough to be the distraction he'd called for. It had worked!

Artan dropped to his front again and unloaded the next magazine into the corner of the wall.

The army's steps closed in from one side, the diseased from another. They were all responding to his attack on the wall.

Artan unloaded his last magazine, discarded his gun, and crawled away from the mound as the front runners in the diseased horde charged towards the soldiers.

Dragging his bag of magnets and his bag of clean clothes for Nick with him, Artan remained on his front and slithered over the damp grass, the diseased mob and army now behind him.

The hammering and uneven steps of the creatures beat against the ground like war drums announcing a hellish army. Their shrill battle cry met the stuttered burst of bullet fire. Artan pressed up from the ground and lifted his head above the grass. All the diseased had passed him. He clambered to his feet, rolled his shoulders so his and Nick's spear sheaths sat more comfortably, and ran.

CHAPTER 26

Gracie ran into the cover of the forest first, William a few steps behind her. She slowed her pace and picked her path through the dense press of trees, holding her spear ahead of her, feeling for any obstructions. Leaves crunched beneath her steps. Twigs snapped. The first signs of a new day had lightened the sky before they entered the forest, but the thick canopy threw them into almost complete darkness as if they'd gone back in time by several hours.

"Shit!" A sharp pain stabbed Gracie's right shoulder from where she walked into the end of a branch. She rubbed where it hurt. "So much for using my spear to feel the way!"

"You okay?" William said.

"Yeah. It's only a branch."

"Better than a diseased."

"Tell me about it. I could do wi—"

"What the …?" William said.

Gracie stopped in her tracks. It might have been darker in the forest than out in the meadow, but not so dark it hid the cottage and its pile of diseased corpses from view.

"Shit!" William knocked her left shoulder when he charged toward the cottage. "Tilly?"

"Will you keep it down?" Gracie looked around. For what good it did. If there were diseased or worse in the forest, she'd only see them when they were too close to avoid.

"Tilly!" Quieter this time, William drew his sword, shoved the steel door open, and vanished inside.

A step behind him, Gracie balked before she entered. The reek of dead diseased hung in the air. There were close to twenty of the vile things stacked up along the front of the wonky building like firewood. In a day or two, their stench would carry for miles. Although, a festering pile of diseased in this world aroused little suspicion. Maybe it would be good camouflage. It might allow them to wait here for as long as they liked. Gracie laid her palm over her mum and dad's wedding rings at her chest before gripping her spear with both hands and following William into the house.

"Tilly?" William called from one of the cottage's derelict bedrooms.

Gracie could have told him Matilda had gone the second he'd shoved the door open. Were anyone left, they would have bolted it from the inside. They'd left the torch on the window ledge. She picked it up and flicked it on. Dark and glistening stains dotted the sandy floor. The vinegar reek of rot was stronger in here than the stench coming from the stacked corpses.

A message on the wall. Gracie read it with the aid of her torch's beam. William joined her from the other room, and although he could have done it himself, she read aloud, "Gone to help Artan and Nick. Be back soon."

"Shit!" William said. "What do you think's happened?"

"I dunno, but it sounds like they weren't worried when they wrote it. Or they didn't want us to worry."

"So what do we do?"

"Can we do anything other than wait?"

"I think we should go after them."

"Where?"

"To find Artan and Nick."

"And where *exactly* are Artan and Nick?"

William's cheeks puffed out.

"See my point?"

William shrugged.

"And what if we miss them when they're on their way back? What if we pass each other in the vast dark expanse outside the forest? At least if we stay put, they'll know where to find us. I can't see how us leaving this place will be a help to anyone. Including us." Gracie bolted the door.

William paced back and forth, stepping in the damp patches of blood.

"I'm all ears if you have a better suggestion?" Gracie said.

"No." William shook his head. "I don't."

"Then we wait. We rest. We get our strength up so we might better deal with whatever's thrown at us next."

William continued to pace the room.

"We still have a fight ahead of us," Gracie said. "You need to make sure you take this chance to be ready for it. I know you can't rest your mind right now, but you can rest your body. Sit down."

William sat cross-legged beside her on a dry patch of floor. He released a hard sigh. "I just hate not knowing."

"I know," Gracie said. She slipped free of the four water bladders she had strapped to her and placed them at her feet. She waited for William to do the same with his and turned the torch off.

At first, they sat in total darkness. But Gracie's eyes adjusted, small slithers of light from the holes in the canopy finding their way into the gloomy cottage. Better to sit in the darkness and keep a low profile. "But that's life."

"Huh?" William said.

"Not knowing," Gracie said. "That's life. Especially this life. The only thing we can be certain of is that nothing will go as we planned."

"Including climbing the wall?"

"Something will go wrong. That doesn't mean we won't get over it."

"We can be certain of death," William said.

Gracie released an approximation of a laugh with a snort. "Thanks again, by the way."

"For what?"

She laid her hand on her chest. The lump of her mum and dad's rings pressed into her palm. "For helping me get the rings."

"It was luck really."

"But it was your luck. So thank you for sharing it with me." The trees swished outside; the place alive, the elements its puppeteer.

"What was her name?"

"My mum?" Gracie said.

"Yeah."

"Rose."

"Pretty name."

"She was a pretty lady. Smart too. And kind. Unless ..." Gracie paused, her chest rising with her inhale. "Unless you were Aus. I find it hard to believe she was as cruel as he said."

"We all see things from our own perspective. I was an only child, so I have no one to compare with, but I've been close to Artan and Matilda for a long time, and if you asked them to describe their mum independently of one another, you'd get descriptions of two completely different women."

"And their dad?"

"Oh, they were agreed on that. Hard not to be."

"How so?"

"He was a sadistic arsehole. A nasty bastard. He's better off dead. And I don't say that lightly, or without Tilly and Artan's complete blessing."

"And what about you? Your mum? Your dad?"

"I was lucky. I was close to them both. Dad especially. We had a tight bond. It was hard going on national service and even harder coming back."

"The whole of Edin had fallen by then, right?"

William stared straight ahead, his profile a silhouette in the darkness. The light caught the glaze in his unfocused eyes, the bob of his Adam's apple. "Yeah, and so many people with it. I went back home. I knew it was hopeless, but I needed to see that for myself." He picked up a water bladder and took a sip.

"You don't want to talk about it?"

William took another sip. "No, not right now."

CHAPTER 27

Olga had one full magazine in her gun. When spent, her weapon would be no more than a glorified club. At that point, she'd do better to take her chances with her sword. She led the way through the dark forest. Every hair on her body stood on end as if reading the slightest fluctuations in her environment. Matilda walked at the back, and they had Hawk between them. He bore Nick's weight and a bag of magnetic handles. They closed in on the small abandoned building. The windows were dark. The door closed. The diseased remained piled up out the front. Had William and Gracie still not made it back?

"What happened here?" Nick said, his voice weak.

Eighteen dead diseased on my doorstep. Hawk had only sung it once, but that once had drilled the tune into Olga's brain.

"Eighteen d—"

"Don't!" Olga cut him off. "It's a long story," she said. "Let's get you inside so you can rest." She pushed against the cold door, but it didn't open. The stock of her barrel resting into her shoulder, she looked down the barrel and knocked.

Clack! Someone freed the bolt, pulled the door wide, and blinded Olga with a bright light. She pointed her gun at them, her finger on the trigger.

"Olga, it's me!" The light dropped so it shone on her boots. "It's Gracie."

"And William." He slipped outside and helped Hawk carry Nick back into the cottage. He sat Nick down and hugged Matilda.

Olga entered the cottage last. One final glance back out into the dark forest. No diseased yet. She closed the door behind them.

"What happened?" Gracie said.

"Quite a lot," Olga said. "Did you get the rings?"

Laying her palm to her chest, Gracie nodded. "Yeah, I did. What happened to Nick?"

"And where's Artan?" William said.

The door swung open before Olga could fully shut it. She raised her gun again, snapping it into her shoulder. Gracie's torch lit him up. "Artan!" Olga said. "How did it go?"

"Okay." He looked behind him. "I think." *Crunch!* He dropped the bag of magnets and carried his smaller bag to Nick's side. "I have clean clothes both for you to wear and for us to use as bandages."

Olga locked the door behind him.

Nick drew shallow breaths, his face glazed with a sheen of sweat.

"I'm sorry," Artan said, "but this is going to hurt. Raise your arms."

Following Artan's instructions, Nick winced and trembled. He stretched up to the ceiling while Artan slowly rolled his top from him. The green shirts Artan had used to dress his wounds were soaked with blood.

"We have water," Gracie said. She handed a full bladder to

Artan. "To clean his wounds." She passed another one to Olga.

Olga unscrewed the lid, took a sip, and passed it on. It quenched her thirst, but left a muddy taste. She turned away from Nick's wounds. Not that she could unsee the deep lacerations covering his torso. Hopefully, if they cleaned them now, they'd keep out infection.

Nick dragged air in through gritted teeth when Artan poured water on him. "I'm sorry again, Nick. I screwed up and blamed you for it."

"Honestly," Nick said, dragging in another sharp intake of breath, "it's fine. Either of us could have blown our cover. We were unlucky, that's all."

"I'm sorry I don't have your grace."

Nick winked, his smile crooked. "I can teach you that."

"They don't look as deep as I first thought," Artan said. He peeled away the final few bandages and discarded them on the floor in a damp pile.

William and Matilda tore the clean clothes Artan had brought for bandages into strips.

Olga shivered to watch the trembling Nick. Colder inside the cottage than out, he sat there soaked and exhausted.

"I think once we have them cleaned and redressed," Artan said, "you'll heal. As long as we can keep out infection."

"Peaches?" Olga said.

Artan and Matilda looked at her, but William spoke first. "Peaches," he said, "I think we're going to stay here forever."

A wry smile, Matilda nodded. "Forever and ever, peaches."

Even Artan grinned.

The others mirrored Olga's scowl. What the hell were they talking about? "Does anyone care to explain?"

"It's a secret code between Artan and myself," Matilda said. "When we use the word peaches, we don't mean what we say afterwards. As in, peaches, I love this cottage so much, I think I want to spend the rest of my life here."

"Peaches," William said, "it's so warm and cosy."

"It was a way to get around my dad's rage," Matilda said. The mood in the room dropped. "He was a control freak and a narcissist, as most of you already know. We had to do exactly what he wanted, when he wanted. You had to say the right thing, and what was right would change from day to day. Most of the time, he played us off against one another. He kept us permanently disorientated."

"If we ever said anything horrible about each other because he forced us to," Artan said, "we'd always say *peaches*. We never meant it. We were just trying to survive, you know?" He reached out to Matilda and momentarily held her hand.

"I'm sorry," Olga said.

Artan shrugged. "He got what was coming to him. And, you know what? We were raised in a chaotic environment. Maybe that's an advantage in this world."

∼

WHILE ARTAN TENDED to Nick's wounds, the rest of them stood with their thoughts. Olga glanced at the window on her left, expecting to see the bleeding eyes of a diseased again.

During Nick's treatment, most of them had turned away. Only so much blood and flesh they could take. But Hawk continued to watch on, standing close by, running his fingers along his own scars. "If only we had some of the ointment from the Asylum."

"Hopefully we can make sure it doesn't get infected," Artan said. He tossed aside yet another empty water bladder. "I'm hoping we've caught it early enough."

The wounds clean, Artan took the strips of fabric from William and Matilda and dressed Nick's cuts. "So what happened out there?" He flicked his head towards the front door. "With the diseased?"

Olga glanced at the window again. The early morning light penetrated the thick forest. No silhouettes outside.

"They found us in the cottage," Matilda said.

"Say it like it is, Matilda." Olga pointed at herself. "I screwed up. I made too much noise and brought them down on us. I was getting antsy and raised my voice too loud. Of course they were going to turn up."

"We've been through a lot in a short space of time," William said. "I'm glad we're all back together now."

"Yeah." Matilda reached out and held his hand. "Now we need to give Nick some time to heal."

Hawk said, "How much time?"

Olga added, "And are we still going to go south?"

Wrapping the last of the bandages around Nick, Artan nodded at the bag of magnets he'd brought with him. "Seems like a waste if we don't. After what we went through to get them. What do you say, Nick?"

The back of his head resting against the wall, his eyes closed to slits, Nick said, "You think I'm going to go through all the shit we've been through and then decide to go north?"

"So you're still up for it?" William said.

"Yes. Of course. When?"

"I think first light will be the best time," Artan said. "Use the light to help us climb and hopefully get over the wall before the guards wake up. They don't always patrol the wall, right, Gracie?"

"I've only ever seen guards on it when they're opening the gates."

"They must be confident in their defences," William said.

Hawk smirked. "Or they think no one's stupid enough to climb it."

"And that's how we'll get them," Artan said.

"By being stupid?"

Artan winked. "Only time will tell."

"But it's first light," Olga said. "It's too soon for you now, right, Nick?"

"But the longer we wait here," Hawk said, "the greater the chance of us being caught. Either by the community we just screwed over, or the diseased. We can help Nick get over the wall. We'll work as a team."

"No." Matilda shook her head. "We don't make that decision for him."

"But we're a team," Hawk said. "We all have a voice."

Swigging from her water bladder, Gracie tossed the empty vessel aside and said, "Let's take a vote on it. Who votes we stay so Nick has time to rest?"

William, Artan, and Matilda raised their hands.

"And go?"

Hawk and Gracie raised theirs. Another glance at the window. Still no bleeding eyes. But how long would it be before they turned up? Olga added her hand to the vote. "We can help Nick with whatever he needs, but I think the sooner we leave, the better."

Nick also raised his hand. "I vote to go too. We can't risk getting caught because of me. And this place stinks!"

"Argh, damn it!" Olga shook her head. "I'm changing my vote. As desperate as I'm sure we all are to leave this place, Nick needs to rest. We didn't give Max the time he needed, and look what happened. Regardless of our motivation to get out of here, we need to honour and support each other's needs. Nick's are currently the greatest. He shouldn't be made to feel bad about that. And, as you said, Gracie, we might never get where we intend to go. We need to make the decisions that honour this moment. And in this moment, our greatest need as a group is to make sure Nick feels up to the task at hand. We'll go out hunting during the day, get some food, rest, and then go out before first light tomorrow. In only twenty-four hours. Agreed?"

Nods passed around the room.

"Is that enough time for you, Nick?" Artan said.

Nick nodded along with them. "I'll make sure it is."

CHAPTER 28

Gracie salivated even while she chewed on the cooked deer. She spoke with her mouth full, the words falling from her before she had the decorum to stop them. "This tastes so good. We really lucked out finding deer south of the ruined city." Even as she chewed, her stomach rumbled, desperate to digest what her senses promised.

William wiped a dribble of fat from his chin. "You didn't eat *any* when you were cooking it?"

"No." She covered her mouth with the back of her hand. "We wanted to wait to share it with you all." Gracie had gone hunting with Hawk and Olga. They'd cooked the meat far from the cottage. They couldn't risk the smoke and the smell attracting unwanted attention.

Artan's cheeks bulged, and he spoke through pursed lips. "Thank you."

Gracie smiled, but Hawk positively beamed. He'd led the hunt. After being shoved aside in Dout like he was no use to them, he'd needed this hunt almost as much as they'd all needed a meal.

For dessert, they had carrots and apples taken from some

spots Dout used to grow their food. It wasn't like anyone else would be needing them.

"We've got no bullets left," Hawk said, raising his gun. He'd eaten while standing and remained mostly in shadow close to the door, the torchlight weaker where he stood. He'd taken it upon himself to be their first line of defence should the bolt fail them. "Is it worth taking the guns with us?"

Gracie, like everyone else, turned to Artan. The man with the plan.

"It's more to carry, and there's no way of knowing if there's any ammo on the other side. And even if there is, will it work in our guns? I say we leave them. Our swords and knives will be much more use. It's the same with the spears. We can make more on the other side, and they're too long to carry while we're climbing."

"Not that we have a choice," Olga said. She sat on the window ledge, her face half hidden in the darkness. She glanced out every once in a while. "You've used them all on the magnets. So what's the plan?"

Artan looked at Nick, who nodded in return. The time he'd taken to rest seemed to have done him good, but not so good he wanted to give them a debriefing about what lay ahead. Artan said, "As Olga's rightly pointed out, we have no spears left. We used them to bind the magnets together in strips of three. We snapped them so they weren't too long."

The sets of handles lay in the room's corner. They'd left them so the magnetic sides rested against the sandy floor. They were strong enough that if they all clamped together, they'd waste a lot of effort separating them again. Not only had Artan run the now broken spears through the handles, but he'd also bound them tight with fabric. The fabric of Nick's used bandages. "Three is enough to support our weight," Artan said. "Any fewer and it won't work, which is why we had to go back into the community to get more.

These handles are strong on their own. They only came free from the doors when we twisted them."

"Which we won't be doing on the wall," Gracie said. "Not with them bound together like that."

"It makes them much safer for our purpose," Artan said.

"So how do we use them?" Olga glanced outside again.

"We'll take two sets each. We stand on one while ..." Artan retrieved a strip of three magnets, held them out in front of him on an invisible wall, and he shifted one side and then the other. "We slowly shuffle the higher of the two sets farther up the wall. They're solid, but they will shift if you move them like this."

"And how do we bring up the lower strip of magnets?" Gracie said.

"We hang on to the higher set with one hand and reach down."

Gracie's stomach flipped.

"You're sure they'll hold?" Hawk said.

"They did when we tried them on the wall of the community we've just left." He pointed his thumb at Nick. "We both climbed to the top of the wall and avoided a horde of diseased when they ran past us. The magnets held us in place just fine. In fact, it took quite an effort to prize them off the wall again when we came back down."

"If they're that strong," Gracie said, "why do you need them in strips of three?"

"Two didn't hold our weight. When we tried, we slowly slid down the wall."

"But the wall you tested these magnets on is a tenth of the size of the one we have to climb," Olga said.

Artan's eyes pinched. "Does magnetic force diminish the higher you climb?"

"No, but my willingness to trust it does."

And Gracie's too.

"Artan," Matilda said, "if you've tried them and you're happy they work, then I'm prepared to give it a go."

"And me," William said.

Hawk said, "I'll give it a go too."

Olga's brow wrinkled. "Fine." She shrugged. "Whatever."

Gracie could have done with someone on her side. Did they all seriously think this would work? "What about the sentry guns?"

Artan said, "Surely they're just for shooting things on the ground? Also, if they have sensors, those sensors have to have blind spots."

"So we climb over really close to them?"

"Yeah." Artan nodded. "And I'm hoping we might be able to disable them when we get near. Reach inside and break them."

"Hoping?" Gracie said.

"Without a working model in front of us, hope is the best we have. And if the guns prove to be a problem, we'll climb over where the guards gather above the gates."

Gracie's quickening pulse shook her words. "We're going to climb over that close to them?"

"That's why we're going to leave here when it's dark and climb up during first light. We'll be over before anyone sees us. And we know the guns on top of the wall don't target the guards, so if it comes to it, that's the route we take. Unless you have a better plan B?"

Olga continued to stare out of the window. Hawk chewed on an apple. Nick leaned his head back against the wall and closed his eyes.

"If anyone has any better suggestions, I'm willing to listen," Artan said.

"What about Nick?" Gracie said.

Nick opened his eyes. "What about me?"

"Let's not kid ourselves. If we're going to climb that wall

soon, you'll need our help. We can speculate on a lot of things about what lies ahead, but pretending you won't need some assistance seems naïve. So we either wait here for you to fully heal, or we need to know how we can help you."

"I can climb up on one side of Nick," Matilda said, "and Artan can climb up the other. We can lift his magnets for him."

"You don't want to wait any longer?" Gracie said.

Nick shook his head. "The longer we wait here, the greater the chance of someone finding us. I think we've ridden our luck by waiting for just one more day."

"And if it doesn't work?"

"It will," Artan said.

"You'd bet your life on it?"

"I'm about to. And if we get ten feet from the ground and it feels wrong, then we come back and think of another plan. However we scale this wall, it won't be easy. And, like I've said, if you have any other suggestions, I'm all ears."

Gracie shrugged. She couldn't predict how this would turn out. She could only honour this moment. She pressed her palm over the rings at her chest. The rings William had risked his life to help her retrieve. They could adapt if things went wrong. And what would she do, anyway? Start a life on her own in this mess of a world?

"Okay," William said, "let's all get as much rest as we can. Olga, are you okay keeping watch for now?"

Olga nodded.

"We'll take turns at the window to give you a break." William turned the torch off, throwing them into complete darkness. "We leave just before first light."

CHAPTER 29

"Just before first light. The best time to sleep. The best time to be woken. Yes, the best time to be woken." She nodded, her hair falling across her face. Swiping it away, she tucked it behind her right ear. "The best time for Joni to wake him. The worst time for him." She smiled. "The absolute worst time for him. Break his rest. Steal his sleep. Wake him up before the birds sing. Ha! What birds? Why would we get birds here? Why would anything living choose to come here? There is no life here. Only death. Slow, sad, and depressing death." Her whisperings echoed in the maintenance shaft. Hyper-acoustics created by the steel walls in the tight crawlspace. But they died out before they went too far. She didn't speak loud enough to get caught. She'd been doing this for too long to get caught. "Too long."

Her backpack was filled with food and clothes. She rolled her shoulders to re-centre it. Crawling through the tunnels always upset the balance of a loaded backpack. "But worth it. With such a plentiful bounty and such easy pickings, Joni can cope with a small amount of discomfort. A heavy reminder of what she'd stolen from them. Again."

Joni came to the section where six maintenance tunnels intersected. The one that went up to the next floor allowed her to stand. She stretched, rolled the aches from her shoulders, and reached up over the ledge in front of her.

"It's still here. With miles of tunnels, how will they ever find Joni's hiding spots? How will they ever find Joni?" She smiled. Dark laughter bubbled in her throat like boiling tar. "They won't!"

Joni retrieved the adjustable spanner and the small foil tray. She'd cut out a thin layer of sponge and laid it along the tray's base a long time ago. It remained, the top covered in a green layer of mould. She pressed it, leaving an impression of her finger in the earthy sludge. "Still flexible enough. And still damp from the last time. Oh, how he screamed." She grinned so wide her cheeks hurt. "How he screamed!"

Dropping back down onto all fours, Joni crawled along the tunnel. They'd made most of the maintenance shafts from solid steel, but they had open vents facing the rooms below. Better for the air circulation. And better for getting at those who needed to be got.

And there he lay. Asleep in his bed. As he should be. Before first light. The best time to be asleep. The most restful hours. "The best time to be woken." Joni giggled again before reaching up to the pipe above her. She tightened the spanner on the bolt and positioned the tray with the layer of sponge beneath it.

She turned the spanner. "Just a short turn. The smallest amount. A drip, drip, drip. Maddening. Enough. Not overkill. Joni has control here, not him. Joni controls the water. She controls his sleep." The steady drip landed in the tray, hitting the green layer of slime on the mouldy sponge base with a slight *tick*.

"But not enough for him to hear. Quiet like Joni. In control."

The man in the room beneath her slept alone in a double bed. "Hopeful. Like he'd get anyone to join him. A cretin of a man. Hatred and malicious intent run through his veins." Balding, he had ginger hair around the sides and back of his head. He had pasty white skin and a bloated face. "Like one of them. Like a diseased. But not as smart. Stupid man." She spat the words. "Stupid. Stupid. Stupid."

Joni pulled away, crawling backwards along the tunnel. Back the way she'd come from. When she'd laid the sponge along the base of the foil tray, she'd also tied a small piece of string to one edge so she could reel it in like a fish. She laid the string along the maintenance tunnel's floor, tracing her retreat.

Back at the point where the tunnels intersected, Joni stood up and replaced her spanner. She crouched back down, her backpack heavy on her shoulders. Heavy with their food. "Joni's food now."

She pulled on the piece of string, whipping the small metal dish away from the drip. "Drip. Drip. Drip."

Within seconds, he screamed. It rang through the building. Through the maintenance tunnels. "He'll wake the entire place. They'll be mad. Oh, so mad. But not as mad as him. Not as mad as Joni has made him. Joni could have cut his throat a thousand times over. Snuck in, taken his life, and left. But that would have been too simple." She smiled again and continued to wind in the small tray. "Too simple."

Thunk!

Joni spun around. A light behind her. "They've responded fast this time." But even if she didn't choose the tunnel where she'd loosened the pipe, or the tunnel they approached from, she still had four escape routes.

"Huh?"

Joni tugged the string again. But the foil tray had caught in the maintenance tunnel. "No." Joni shook her head.

The people behind were in the shafts with her.

"No. They're coming. They can't find the tray. They can't know Joni has been here. Joni can't give the game away. Not now. Not after all these years."

She tugged the string again, but the foil tray remained stuck.

"Oh no, Joni. You've gone and blown it. No." She shook her head. She needed to go in any direction other than towards the tray or the people.

"Your only choice, Joni. You can't leave the tray. Go and get it. Take it with you. Bring it back next time. Yes! You can bring the tray back next time. Clean it maybe? Replace the sponge. Make it even quieter. Drip, drip."

Joni crawled on all fours ahead of the people towards the snagged tray. "Joni's faster than all of them along these tunnels. This is Joni's world, and they're just visitors."

She passed over the tray and scooped it up. "Remove the evidence." She continued on, the drip hitting the back of her head when she passed beneath it. The man paced the room below. She should have cut his throat years ago. But that would have been too quick. Too easy. He didn't deserve easy.

Joni reached the end of her tunnel and turned right. She paused and peered back the way she'd come from. The people behind came into view. Just one person. The man shouted to him from below, "What's going on up there?"

"We have a leak," the maintenance man said.

"I know we have a fucking leak! That's what woke me."

"Joni woke you. Joni will always wake you. Steal from you. Cut your throat. No, no, she won't cut your throat. Too fast. Too easy."

"Has it stopped?" the maintenance man said.

"Yeah."

"Okay. It's fixed."

"But why does it keep happening?"

"I can only tell you what I see," the maintenance man said. "And I've fixed it to the best of my ability."

"But why so many leaks?" he said. "It's like this place knows where I am and breaks around me."

"You've spent a lot of time in here."

"Are you saying I'm going mad?"

Covering her mouth, Joni giggled. "Mad, yes. Much slower than a cut throat."

"No, sir," the maintenance man said. "But your time in this place has increased your chances of being a victim to coincidence, which would, understandably, make you want to place a narrative on those random events."

"I'm making it up?"

"No, sir. They're happening."

"Then what?!"

"I wish I had answers for you, but I don't. I'm sorry."

"Joni needs to get away from here. Joni's had her fun. She can't get carried away. She can't blow her cover. No. That wouldn't end well." As she crawled off, the men continued arguing behind her. The evidence that she'd been there removed from the scene. "Joni moves through this place like poison gas. Carbon monoxide, she'll kill you in your sleep. No." She hit her head with the heel of her right hand. "Not kill you. Make you ill." She smiled. "Joni will make you very, very ill." She laughed again. "Joni doesn't want you to die, she wants you to suffer forever."

CHAPTER 30

The foggy darkness buried much of their surroundings save for the thick bar of the wall ahead. Taller than the low-lying weather, it stood as their destination. The group remained close enough to see one another. Close enough for Artan to make out the beads of sweat on Nick's brow. The dark bags beneath his eyes. The wincing with every step. They'd left too soon. They should have stayed in the cottage longer and taken their chances until he recovered.

Both of Artan's arms ached from carrying his and Nick's magnets. Six large handles in each grip, two bars of three. He gripped hard to prevent them from pulling face to face. Not impossible to separate, but a struggle they didn't need when they reached the base of the wall. At least the weather benefited them. Nature's camouflage aiding their journey. And they could climb to a decent height while cloaked in fog. And at least Nick could walk unaided. "How are you doing?"

"That's about the tenth time you've asked me," Nick said. The muscles in his jaw tensed, and he gritted his teeth. "And for the tenth time, I'm fine."

"You sure you're ready for this? You don't think we should head back to the cottage?"

"Are *you* ready?"

Olga snapped around and scowled at Artan. And she had a point. He needed to shut up. They might have been well-hidden, but the fog didn't mute them. Dropping his voice to a whisper, he said, "I'm sorry. I'm just worried about you. You wouldn't be in this state had I not screwed up."

"And I appreciate your concern," Nick said. "But please trust me when I say I'm more than capable of advocating f—" He drew a sharp intake of breath, held his right arm across his front, and paused mid-step. "For myself."

Artan pushed his lips tight against his desire to respond. Little point in arguing about it now.

"Shit!" Olga said.

The low snarl of a diseased in the fog ahead. Further proof the fog didn't mute them. Had it heard Artan?

The ring of steel. The *thunk* of magnets hitting the ground. William, Matilda, and Olga all carried swords and moved to the front of the group.

Artan stepped across Nick to protect him.

Olga lunged into the fog. Her sword sank with a *squelch*, and the diseased fell with a *thud.*

Gracie said, "Is that all o—"

Wild. Unhinged. Shrill. Another diseased burst forward.

William skewered their chest. He impaled them and then kicked them backwards, the air leaving them with a hiss as they crumpled. Matilda finished them by stabbing them in the face before she took down the next creature on her upswing.

Artan placed his and Nick's magnets face down on the damp grass. He drew his knife as he moved closer to their attackers. He should have kept at least one spear.

Lunging into the fog, William pulled back and said, "Stop!" He cupped his ear. "Listen."

They all paused.

The snarling and phlegmy death rattle of diseased respiration had vanished. But distant footsteps galloped towards them.

"Shit," Olga said again. "It sounds like there're hundreds of the bastards."

"It always sounds worse when you can't see them," Artan said. "Right?" How would he protect Nick against a horde? "Right?" He slipped his knife back into the small sheath at his hip. "What do we do?" He picked up the magnets, two bars of three in each hand. "We can't afford to get caught by that lot."

"You go." Olga pointed away from them. "Take Nick. We'll catch up."

"It's too dark and foggy," Gracie said. "We shouldn't separate from one another. It sounds like there are too many of them to fight. But they haven't seen us yet. That's our advantage. If we're quiet, we can get away from here."

"To where?" Olga said. "Like you said, it's too dark and foggy."

"So, what? We wait here?" Gracie said.

"That might not be such a bad idea," Artan said.

Olga scowled at him. "What are you talking about?"

"If we run, we'll make a noise. But if we walk quietly and move to a different spot, even only one hundred feet away from here, we can continue to hide in the fog."

Olga shook her head. "And you think that'll work?"

"I *hope* it will work. It's better than fighting them. And it's better than running blind."

"I think it's a good idea," William said.

Matilda nodded. "I do too."

And Nick could cope with moving one hundred feet away.

"So we're agreed?" Artan said.

The others picked up their magnets. Olga's slouched frame suggested she didn't have the same enthusiasm for the plan as the rest of them, but she went along with it. And it wasn't like she'd offered anything better.

CHAPTER 31

Thirty minutes of hiding in the fog while the day grew progressively lighter. Olga, like the others, stood still, taking slow breaths, shifting her weight from one foot to the other. Impatience surged through her veins. The diseased around them were going nowhere. And why would they? They had nowhere else to go, and they had idle minds. They either chased prey, or they meandered, wandering around until they were presented with something to chase. They could either wait for the front gates to open and drag the diseased away, which could happen in the next five minutes, the next five hours, or even the next five days, or they could wait for the day to get brighter, for the sun to burn the fog away, and for them to be revealed to the diseased. Neither option ended well. Artan had been right to worry about Nick. He didn't have an escape in him.

Another diseased silhouette stumbled through the fog. Not the first one to get near enough for them to see it, but it hadn't yet seen them. Surely just a matter of time until one stumbled too close? Olga held her two strips of three magnets in her left hand and her sword in her right. She pointed her weapon in the diseased's direction. If it moved closer, she could silence it before it raised the alarm.

The diseased turned away. They got lucky this time. But how long would that luck last? They needed to take charge of their own destiny.

Olga moved close to Gracie. "We need a plan."

"We need to wait."

"But at some point, waiting won't work for us. It'll be daylight. So if we wait, what are we waiting for?"

"The right moment to move," Gracie said.

"But that moment hasn't yet come," Olga said. "At what point do we accept it won't?"

"I don't know." Gracie shook her head. "But fighting won't get us out of this."

"Max would have gotten us out of this."

"But we don't have Max."

"You think I don't know that?"

"I'm not trying to antagonise you, Olga. What I mean is we don't have that option now. We have to do things differently."

"And I intend to." Olga held her magnets in Gracie's direction. "Will you take these to the wall for me?"

"What are you going to do?"

"We're going to climb up on the left side of the gates, right?"

"What are you going to do, Olga?"

"I'll meet you on the wall. To the left of the gates. The only thing I ask is that you get there before me."

"What are you doing?"

"It's like you said, we don't have Max. We have to do things differently. The diseased would have ignored Max. They won't ignore me."

Olga slid her sword back into its sheath and sprinted away from the group, the air cold in her throat. The fog turned to a chilled layer of condensation on her skin. Droplets formed on her eyelashes. She passed diseased. Several of them snorted and growled. The confused sounds of inquisition. Had something just passed them? What was happening?

At least one hundred feet between her and her friends, Olga shoulder barged a diseased. Its arms flailed as it spun away from her. A rancid shot of rot and vinegar remained in the space it had occupied. "Come on, you bastards!"

The diseased responded with a rallying call of their own.

"Woot! Woot!" Olga shouted.

The creatures roared and gave chase.

The ground was soft and uneven. If Olga didn't fall and break an ankle, she might just get away from them. Gracie had best have gotten them moving.

Olga ducked the swiping and atrophied arms of a diseased that charged towards her. The crack of one body hitting another as it slammed into the stampede on her tail.

Ducking right, Olga avoided the next diseased. She ducked left. Each time, she avoided the imminent danger while the pack swelled in number behind her. But she needed more of them. She needed *all* of them so the others could move on. "This is for you, Max!" It hurt her throat to shout. "This is for you!" They'd best be ready for her when she reached the wall.

CHAPTER 32

They had to be ready for her for when she needed to climb the wall. After what Olga had just done for them, Gracie couldn't let her down. She'd failed an entire community. Hopefully, even she could facilitate the needs of just one person. Holding her and Olga's magnets stretched the grips on both hands to their limit. Streaking pains ran the length of her fingers. She scanned their surroundings. Their visibility was still poor, but the day had grown brighter. Would the fog hide them all the way to the wall?

Gracie tried to engage her core as she walked down the steep hill, but every step slammed through her, jarring her knees. She planted one foot, made sure it would hold, and then planted the next. She turned sideways and angled her feet into the slope. It gave her a better grip.

Artan had split his and Nick's magnets between Matilda, William, and Hawk. Hard enough descending this hill alone, but to do it while supporting someone in Nick's state … How would he cope with the climb? It seemed impossible. But Gracie couldn't make that decision for him. They needed to take this one step at a time. Deal with what lay directly in front of them. They'd face the dilemma of the wall when they reached it.

At the bottom of the hill, the urge to run fired through Gracie's twitching legs. The fog might be hiding the diseased, but it hadn't removed them from existence. She settled her raging pulse with deep breaths, expelling clouds of condensation as she walked towards the wall.

The others followed Gracie's lead. She knew this place better than any of them. They were relying on her. It was like they hadn't seen what had happened the last time a group of people did that.

Nick pulled away from Artan and walked unaided. If he could do that, then maybe he'd be okay climbing the wall. Artan took back his and Nick's magnets. Like Gracie, he now carried four strips of three.

Canted silhouettes stumbled through the fog. They appeared and vanished, each one far enough away to avoid. The rolling white clouds swirled around Gracie and laid pinpricks of cold water against her skin. Her nose ran and tingled on its way to turning numb. A hard sniff would go off like an explosion, so she wiped it with the back of her sleeve. The fog might have temporarily blinded the diseased, but they weren't deaf.

Slow and deliberate steps towards the wall, Gracie carried her caution with her from the hill. The creatures screeched and wailed. Snarled and hissed.

One appeared on Gracie's right about ten feet away. A woman, about Gracie's height, but skinny with malnutrition. One arm hung loose, and her crimson glare fixed on Gracie. An inquisitive growl rumbled in her throat.

Gracie's hand tightened on the magnets. The best weapon she had right now.

But the diseased woman remained still. She continued to stare in Gracie's direction. The others, like Gracie, waited.

A squall in the distance. The beast spun so fast, her limp arm swung out with her sharp turn. She ran off, consumed by the fog like she'd never been there.

"Their sight must be awful in this fog." Matilda spoke in a whisper. "That's something at least."

Gracie swallowed a dry gulp and nodded. She pointed in the direction they were heading and led them on again.

~

THE MAGNETS CONNECTED to the brushed-steel barrier with a *thunk!* The first set the loudest, Gracie attached the next with a little more finesse, fighting the magnetic tug. The fog had left a damp layer on the cold steel. Hopefully, the rough surface would provide enough grip.

Artan, Matilda, William, and Hawk all placed their magnets on the wall. A final set on the end for when Olga rejoined them. "Here's hoping it works, eh?" Gracie said.

Artan said, "It'll work. Right, Nick, you get on first."

Did he really have it in him? Sure, he'd walked from the bottom of the hill, but walking along flat ground and climbing as high as they needed to climb ... The back of Gracie's neck ached, and it made her dizzy to look up the length of the wall.

Nick stepped onto the lower magnets, reached up for the higher bar, and clung on. Both sets held.

A demonstration for the others, Artan and Matilda stepped up onto their magnets on either side of Nick. Matilda, on Nick's right, pulled up her side of Nick's foot bar while Nick hung from the higher hand bar, the soles of his boots braced against the damp wall. Artan did the same with the left side.

Nick stepped on the bar again, which now sat six inches higher than it had before.

Artan, with Nick's assistance, raised the left side of the higher set of magnets. Matilda then did the same. Six inches at a time, but if they persevered, they'd get there. Hopefully, before the fog cleared.

Artan held onto his own hand bar with one hand, reached down to his foot bar, braced against the wall with the soles of his boots, lifted one side and then the other. While standing on the raised bar, he raised the higher set of handles. Like Nick, he'd lifted himself by six inches. Slow and steady. What else did they have?

∼

AFTER ABOUT TWENTY MINUTES, they were already about a quarter of the way up the wall. Fifty feet from the ground, Gracie's stomach lurched every time she peered down. The point of no return. They were all in. Fall now and they were screwed. It wouldn't even be worth going after someone if they dropped.

Nick managed with Artan and Matilda's help. Hawk and William had both offered to take over on either side of him, but Artan refused, and Matilda had stamina for days. If only Aus had seen that. Olga and Matilda would have been better assets than half the men in his crew.

Gracie stopped climbing. The others got about five feet higher before they also stopped. Hawk said, "Are you okay?"

"I'm going to wait for Olga. I don't want her to feel like we've left her behind."

The others halted their climb. "You can all carry on. I'll catch you up."

Hawk flicked his head at Artan and Matilda. "You two continue up with Nick. We can move faster. We'll catch up."

Artan nodded and returned to helping Nick. He lifted the foot bar on his side, waited for Matilda to do the same, and then lifted the hand bar. One side and then the next, they continued up the wall.

"You go with them," Gracie said to William. She saved him the dilemma. And of course he should be with Artan and Matilda. Olga didn't need them all waiting with her.

Climbing to be closer to Hawk, the wind stronger now they were higher up, Gracie said, "Thanks for waiting with me."

Hawk shrugged and squinted against the breeze. His face glistened with the damp fog, and his nose had turned red. "You'd do the same. We're in this together, and you're right, it's important Olga doesn't feel abandoned."

"Although, from this high up"—Gracie's stomach flipped again when she looked at the ground—"she is kind of on her own."

"She'd be pissed if it were any other way. And who wants to be on the end of a berating from her? She's fierce."

Gracie smiled. "She is."

The day had grown progressively lighter, and the fog had thinned. The diseased still existed as shambling silhouettes that were yet to notice Gracie and her friends on the wall. But where she'd only seen five or six at once when she'd been on the ground, the brightening day and her elevated position improved her visibility to where she saw all the way back to the steep hill. A hundred or more diseased wandered aimlessly.

"Is that her?" Hawk said.

The silhouette jumped from the top of the hill, hit the slope hard, and rolled. While maintaining her momentum, Olga burst from a roll and got to her feet, bouncing and leaping with the sharp decline. Her arms windmilled as she fought for balance.

"Damn!" Gracie said.

Hawk laughed. "It almost looks fun."

Diseased followed her over. Every one of them lost their balance. "You were saying?" Gracie said.

Olga reached the bottom of the hill and broke into a sprint. Many of the diseased had overtaken her on the way down, but not a single one had found their feet at the bottom. Too broken from the fall. Too disorientated.

While Gracie tracked Olga's mazy run through the beasts between them and the hill, the creatures only stirred once she'd passed them.

At the bottom of the wall, Olga leaped onto the magnets Gracie had left her.

"Shit!" Gracie said. "No one's shown her how to do it."

Before Hawk replied, Olga took to the technique. She pulled the bottom bar up, stood on it, and pushed the top bar. Methodical. Quick. Strong. She scaled the wall like she'd invented the method. She ascended it like a mechanical spider.

∽

Wild eyes, her face glistening with a sheen of sweat, Olga pulled level with Gracie and Hawk.

Gracie shook her head. "You mad bastard."

Olga fought for breath. "Tell me—" she paused "—that wasn't exactly what we needed to get up this wall?"

"Welcome back, Olga," Hawk said.

Olga winked at him. Squinting against the elements, the sun growing brighter, she said, "I had to keep slowing down and making a lot of noise so the diseased stayed with me." She hung away from the wall, turned, and looked at the creatures below.

Gracie's stomach turned backflips, and the backs of her knees tingled.

"I don't think a single one can see us right now," Olga

said. "Although, I don't think it will be long before this fog's cleared." She looked up the wall at the others. They were already about halfway up. A hundred feet from the ground. A long way to fall.

"If you're right about the guards only patrolling when they open the gates," Olga said, "hopefully we can get to the top of this wall unseen. Come on, let's get a move on before someone spots us."

CHAPTER 33

Artan's arms tingled with pins and needles, and his hands throbbed. He hung his right hand down and shook it, an electric buzz running the length of his arm to his fingertips. When the feeling returned, he swapped his grip around and did the same with his left. They were about three-quarters of the way up the wall, clear of the diseased, and despite the new day burning away some of the fog, the creatures one hundred and fifty feet below remained oblivious to their presence.

Every time he moved one of Nick's bars, Artan gave him the same warning. "Moving now."

As he'd done for most of the climb, Nick remained silent, adjusted his weight to help either Artan or Matilda, depending on which one moved his bars at that moment, and allowed them to slowly move him up the wall.

They were above the fog, the steel wall now much drier. The magnets had slid a bit too easily at several points lower down, but they now took more effort to shift. Both a blessing and a curse. A hard gust of wind slammed into Artan, swaying him where he clung on. His stomach lurched again as if encouraging him away from the wall. No matter how long they'd been climbing, he hadn't gotten used to the height. A long way to fall. A long way for Nick to fall.

"How are you doing, Nick?"

"Still okay."

"We're nearly there."

Covered in sweat, Nick nodded and adjusted his weight so Tilly could lift her side of his magnets. His eyes had lost focus, and the grey bandages Artan had used had patches of blood shining through them.

He'd told Nick they were nearly there, but they still had to get past the gun turrets. And if they were forced to adopt plan B, they'd have to face the overhang beneath the guards' section to their right. The wall wider at this point than anywhere else, it gave space on top for the patrolling guards. The shape of the wall both a curse and a blessing. Were any guards to arrive now, they'd have no chance of seeing Artan and his friends in their current spot. But would he swap that for a much easier route to the top? He shook his head. He needed to focus on the turrets. No point in giving energy to plan B while they were still working on plan A.

Each turret stood nearly as tall as Artan and had two cannons protruding from it. A cawing crow glided in over the top of them. Its wingspan two to three feet wide, it headed towards the top of the wall and landed on the turret they were also aiming for. Artan laughed. "If only it were—"

The turret to the left of the crow spun, locked onto the bird, and shot. One of the bullets cleaved the bird in two, both parts of its large black body peeling away. They tumbled and turned, hurtling towards Artan and his friends.

White light smashed through Artan's vision from where half of the bird hit him. The dead *thud* echoed through his skull, and his face throbbed like he'd been punched. The creature's remains rolled away from him and vanished into the fog.

Nick grimaced.

"That bad?" Artan said.

Nick nodded.

Holding on with his left hand, Artan pulled his right into his sleeve and used his top to wipe away the mess. He wiped his face and neck. Several fleshy lumps clung to his shirt. When he'd finished, he turned to Nick. "Better?"

Nick's pause said it all.

"Well, there's that plan screwed," Olga said. "So what do we do now?"

"No!" Artan shook his head. "There must be a way. If we come from the bottom of the turret—"

"We'll get shot," Olga said. "We need to go with plan B."

Nick's Adam's apple bobbed with his gulp. The overhang would be a challenge even if he were fully fit. Maybe plan B needed a rethink. Artan shook the pins and needles from his left arm before doing the same with the right.

"Unless you have a better plan?" Olga said.

They'd been climbing for long enough. The bird might have shown them they now had a different finish line, but they were still close. A trickier climb to get past the overhang, but once they were past it, they were safe. As long as they didn't encounter any surprises on the guards' section of the wall.

"Come on," Gracie shifted her high strip of magnetic handles up and across in the direction of the overhang. "We have to climb into the guards' section. It's still early, hopefully there's no one there."

"Or we go to ground and think of some other plan?" Hawk said.

"After climbing all this way? And with all those diseased

down there?" Olga shook her head. "There's no chance I'm going to ground now unless it's on the other side."

"Or unless you fall," Hawk said.

Olga shrugged. "It's a risk I'm prepared to take."

Hawk turned to Nick. "Can you get past the overhang?"

Nick shivered. The wind tore along the surface of the wall.

"Nick?" Artan said.

Nick's focus returned, but he slurred his words. "I think it'll take more effort to go back down than it will to keep going."

Artan glanced at Matilda. She threw a small shrug back at him. Nick had a point.

Matilda followed Gracie's line towards the overhang. She dragged Nick's magnets for his hands up and across.

"Moving now." Artan shoved from his side.

Gracie and Olga led, both of them leaning away with the shape of the wall. Both of them trembled with the clear effort of holding themselves in that position ...

Nick's head wobbled as if it weighed too much for his neck, and Artan's stomach flipped again. He leaned towards him and reached for his back, but Nick held on. The fog now much thinner below them, it hid the pigeon's fall, but it would give them a clearer view of a body hurtling towards the ground.

A red light burst to life above them. They all froze. Olga and Gracie leaned out as if it might give them a better view of their destination. Not that they needed to see. The red lights were on. They all knew what came next.

Artan gripped tighter. His hands sore, he pulled himself into the wall a moment before the siren sounded. A caterwauling whine, so loud it made him dizzy. It called out to diseased far and wide. Hear ye! Hear ye!

"Shit!" Olga said. "What do we do now?"

CHAPTER 34

The overhang forced the top half of Olga's body out by an extra few feet. The strong wind, siren, and distance between her and Gracie to the rest of their group gave her the courage to speak. Hopefully the others wouldn't hear. It helped with Gracie being higher than her on the overhang. She sent her voice up, away from their friends. "This is a bad idea. I don't think all of us will make it, especially not Nick. We've only climbed a fraction of it, and I don't know about you, but I'm not excited about the prospect of continuing."

Her lips tight, Gracie leaned back from the wall and peered down at the others. They were attached to the section between the top of the gates and the overhang. About twenty feet of flush wall leading to this hellish climb.

Thunk!

A freeing lock. The huge gates twitched, wobbled, and broke away from the wall. Inches at a time, the gap down the centre of the vast steel doors parted.

Olga had banked on the surrounding noise keeping her and Gracie's conversation private. It certainly prevented her from hearing William below. His mouth moved, but the wailing siren drilled into her skull and buried his words. William pointed down at the opening gates.

Olga mimicked William's gesture, and Gracie nodded at her suggestion.

Every time Olga shifted her magnets, her stomach turned somersaults. With how she leaned away with the overhang, gravity hung from her like chains, ready to tug her free and drop her like an apple from a tree. Her body trembled more violently than before, and fatigue made her muscles unresponsive. Were it not for Gracie closing in on her from above, she might have frozen altogether.

Gracie kicked one end of her magnetic bar and then the other before she pulled one side and then the other. She repeated the process as if they weren't over one hundred and fifty feet from the ground. Maybe in her mind they weren't. How else would she master the technique?

The red lights flashed above them, adding to Olga's dizziness. She fought to pinpoint her focus on her progress. "We're only a few feet from the ground. The fall will be fine. Nothing to worry about." Feet first and then hands. Feet and hands. Feet and hands.

Off the overhang, Olga's heart beat so fast it ached. Hawk shook his head again, but this time Olga caught parts of what he said. "No way … we don't … can't …" All the while the gates opened beneath them. They parted with a slow inevitability.

Left side. Right side. Left side. Right side. Feet. Hands. Feet. Hands.

William still too far away to hear, but Hawk went back at him again. "You're mad. We don't know what's on the other side."

"Olga, Gracie," William said, "I think we should go through the gates."

Olga nodded. "Absolutely."

Hawk's jaw fell loose. "*What?* But we don't know what's there."

It hurt Olga's throat to speak loud enough to be heard over the siren, so she waited for Gracie to get closer. She didn't need to be repeating herself. "No, we don't, but we know the guns will shoot us if we get too close."

Gracie nodded along with her.

"They might even shoot us if we get to the top of the overhang. And for all we know, there are always guards waiting above us; we just didn't see them from the ground. Also, I hate to say it, but even from the small attempt Gracie and I just made at the overhang, we won't all make it to the top. I pushed Max to do something that was beyond him, and look what happened. I'm not going to do it again with Nick. It's not an easy climb at all. I'm not even sure if I'll make it, and I'm not carrying anywhere near the same injuries. Sorry, Nick."

Nick shrugged.

"And it gets us inside," Gracie said. "Isn't that our goal?"

"You agree with her?" Hawk said.

"If you'd just attempted that overhang, you would too."

The huge steel gates continued to open beneath them. Each one two feet thick.

"It seems like most of you agree with Olga and Gracie?" A raised vein throbbed at Hawk's temple, and his face turned puce with the effort of having a conversation over the screaming chaos.

"What's happening now?" Matilda pointed down.

The gates had pulled far enough from the wall to show them a slither of a view inside. An ever-increasing triangular gap that revealed more of the scenes below. People gathered, waiting for them to open wider. They kicked out at the atrophied arms of the diseased reaching through to them from the other side.

The diseased screamed and whined. The gap grew, an inch at a time. The people inside guarded the space. They kicked through, driving the diseased back.

"If we're going to do this," William said, "we need to do it now. We won't get closer to these opening gates than this."

"Are you ready, Nick?" Artan said.

"Yep."

"Moving now." Artan tugged the left side of Nick's magnetic handles down. Only a few feet above the gates, they wouldn't get a better opportunity.

Matilda helped Nick on the other side.

The people preparing to leave filled the gap as it widened. They stood shoulder to shoulder. They worked as a unit, kicking and shoving, forcing the diseased back.

The people on the ground had a line of robotic dogs behind them. It sent a chill streaking through Olga's veins. The dogs were like the ones they'd seen in the ruined city. A drone zipped over the crowd and vanished from sight again. Maybe they had guns hanging down. From the top, they were similar to the ones they'd already seen.

"This must be where those machines come from," Matilda said, pulling her side of Artan's top handles down. "What are they doing?"

"At a guess." Olga opened and closed her mouth as if it might relieve the pressure on her eardrums from where the siren swelled through her brain. "I'd say they're herding the people. Making sure they don't turn around. They're probably also stopping the diseased entering."

The people below screamed with the same ferocity as their diseased counterparts. They remained locked together at the ever-increasing gap. They fought the creatures. They kicked, punched, and shoved. All the while, the dogs edged closer, forcing them out.

Olga kicked her foot bar down on the left and then on the

right. She tugged the left handle and then the right. Gracie remained a few feet above her.

The people's defence failed. The first diseased burst through. It tackled someone to the ground, its mouth snapping before it sank its teeth into their face.

The panic infected the crowd, and they charged. Several of them found paths through the tight press of bodies. Packs of diseased chased them away from the wall. It opened space for the others.

All the while, the vast gates continued to open.

Olga bounced on her magnetic platform as if she could run for the people still inside. "What are they waiting for? They're not going to get a better chance than this."

"It must be hard to see from their vantage point," Gracie said. "We have a unique view of what's happening."

Many of the dwindling group of people still inside hid behind the partly open gates. Many of the diseased had charged off across the foggy meadow in pursuit of their prey. But their plan had a shelf life. If the dogs didn't force them out first, the opening gates would reveal them soon enough. They continued to part with a slow and steady inevitability.

William reached the top of the opening gates first. Hawk next. Artan and Matilda continued to help Nick down. They were close.

Gracie above her still, Olga froze. A small boy, one of those who'd remained inside the gates, stared up and pointed. His mouth moved, but with chaos unfolding around him, no one paid him any mind. "Shi—"

One of the few diseased still inside the gates slammed into the kid, turning him into a rag doll as it landed on top of him. It raised its face to the sky and bit down hard.

The few people who'd remained inside took their chance and ran out into the meadow. If any of the others had seen Olga and her friends, they clearly had more pressing issues.

Left. Right. Left. Right. Olga made her way to the thick top of the opening gates. Only she and Gracie remained on the wall.

The downed boy twitched and snapped, twisted and writhed. The disease in his veins, he turned on the ground like a crushed spider, fighting to master control of his broken body.

Whomp! One of the dogs lit up the child. An intense blast of fire that first burned his clothes, turned his skin charcoal black, and finally killed his thrashing movements.

A drone shot the remaining diseased, its bullets animating those they caught while several more ran out into the meadow.

Uncertainty might be waiting for them on the other side of the wall, but they were heading that way anyway. And anything had to be better than trying to go over the top. Olga kicked the left side of the magnets and then the right. She pulled down the left and then the right. They were going to reach the gates, but what the hell would they do when they were inside? She couldn't think about that. One step at a time. They were closer to getting past this wall than they'd ever been before. If they were measuring their progress, for now, this had to count as a win.

CHAPTER 35

Gracie hung down and stepped onto the gate on her side. It continued to open. Although slow, she held onto her magnets and felt its momentum before she let go of her magnets. The last one on, she raised her arms. "Yes!"

The gate stopped moving, and Gracie wobbled where she stood. They'd only opened part way. Wide enough to let everyone out. They had no need to open any wider.

Gracie copied the others in dragging her magnets down. The space usually filled by the gates made it much easier to detach them from the wall. She dragged the first strip free and attached them to the inside of the gate before dragging off the second set. She lay across the top of the wall on her front, the steel cold against her stomach, and reached down. She laid the second set of magnets lower than the first. Like they'd done the entire time, they had one set higher for their hands, and one set lower for their feet. It had served them well to this point. Her two magnets formed the final piece in the line of seven sets. They were all ready to move on. To get on the other side of the wall.

One hundred and fifty feet from the ground, Gracie sat

with her friends. A moment's rest, her body thrummed with fatigue. They all needed a minute. The strong wind slammed into her. She filled her lungs with the fresh breeze. Most of the fog had burned away, banished by the bright sun. Of those who'd run from the gates, only a few survivors reached the steep hill they'd descended earlier. The point where their chances of survival increased exponentially.

None of the diseased looked up. And could they even see this high through their bloody glares? And the survivors were clearly too busy surviving to care. The dogs remained as a militant line inside the community. The drones hovered above them. The occasional rattle of bullet fire or *whomp* of igniting flames drove back any inquisitive diseased. But they were no more than that. With no people to chase, the diseased had little reason to enter the gates.

They all needed the rest, but from the way Nick lay sprawled on his back along the thin edge of the gate, he needed it the most. A fish on a riverbank, he gasped and panted, wincing as if even drawing breath caused him pain. Spots of blood stained his grey top, and he sweated like he had a fever. They still had a long way to climb.

The gate shifted, and Gracie threw her arms out to the sides for balance. It rocked and wobbled before both sides slowly closed in again.

"That's us, then," Hawk said. "I knew it wouldn't last. Let's hope this works." He laughed. "If it doesn't, I can genuinely say it's been nice knowing you all."

"Stop that," Matilda said.

Hawk lay across the wall on his front and hung the lower half of his body towards his magnets. His feet swung and missed the lower set several times before he caught them. He then reached under with his hands, grabbed on, and slid from the top of the gate. "Oi," he shouted, "look at this!"

Gracie leaned over with the others. Hawk's magnets were

the closest to the gate's hinge. The closest to the thick wall they were embedded in. "What are we looking at?"

"You can't see it from up there?" Hawk said.

"The gates are closing, Hawk. Now's not the time for a wasted conversation."

"There's an entrance and stairs here. The stairs lead up. I reckon they take us to the guards' section above. I'll go in."

Olga went next. She slid from the gates and clung on to her magnets. Two down. Five of them to go.

The gates continued to close. Slow and steady. Inevitable.

William followed as Olga sidestepped from one set of magnets to the next and followed Hawk into the entrance. At least they had a way out of there.

They were all mobilising to get off the gate, but Nick still hadn't moved.

Gracie waited while Matilda said, "Nick, are you okay? Artan?"

Pale-faced and tight-lipped, Artan shook his head and raised his eyebrows.

"Shit!" Gracie said. They had two options. They either remained on top of the gates until they were shoved off as they closed, shifting them from their perch and throwing them to the ground. Or they got onto their magnets, and quick.

From the way Nick trembled and shook, he didn't have quick in him.

"Tilly," Artan said, "I'm going to get on my magnets, and I want you to slide Nick down so he's between me and the gate. Even if we get to that point and rest, we need to get off this wall."

"Okay." Matilda nodded.

"I'll help," Gracie said. She shifted across to join them. Matilda pressed a hand on Nick that spoke partly of her comforting him, and partly of her pinning him in place so he didn't fall. In his current state, he couldn't be responsible for his own well-being.

Artan clung to the inside of the gate and called up, "Ready when you are."

Matilda climbed over Nick, clearing the way for Gracie to grab the side of him closest to her.

Nick whined when Matilda rolled his flaccid body onto his front. "Have you got him on your side, Gracie?"

Gracie copied how Matilda sat. She dropped one leg over each side of the wide gate, digging into the cold steel with her knees like straddling a horse. She held Nick just below his armpits and let his body weight carry him off the side to Artan.

Her thighs burning from supporting Nick's weight, Gracie let him slip a few inches at a time. All the while, the gates dragged her and Matilda closer to the wall.

Artan leaned away to give Nick the space to slot in front of him. "A few more inches," he said. "Nearly there."

Gracie's entire body shook.

"Nearly there," Artan said.

The gate dragged them closer to the immovable barrier of the flat wall. Gracie said, "How much longer, Artan?"

"Another inch," Artan said. "Got him! You can let go."

Gracie released her grip and spun around so she lay on her front. She clung onto the right-angled edge of the gate farthest away from her, found the lower down magnets with her feet, reached for the higher set with her hands, grabbed them, and slid clear as the gate passed beneath the wall.

The gates were much thinner than the main wall, which allowed the space for Hawk's entranceway. A few sets of magnets between her and the opening, stairs led up and away from their spot. They must have used it for maintenance. They might not have known exactly where it led, but anything had to be better than clinging to these walls for any longer than necessary.

Matilda, who'd also slipped from the top of the gate at the last minute, stared at Gracie with wide eyes. Gracie snorted a laugh. "We did it."

"We did." A rueful smile, Matilda shook her head. "Although I'm not sure how."

The dogs below them turned and walked away. The drones followed. "You know," Gracie said, "we might just pull this o—"

"Shit!" Artan said.

The word struck like lightning, and Gracie froze.

The combined weight of Artan and Nick proved too much for the magnets. Like the opening and closing of the gates, they moved with slow yet inevitable progress as they slid down the wall.

CHAPTER 36

Gracie would have reached down had Matilda not beaten her to it. Her fingers splayed on her right hand as if it would give her the extra few inches she needed to catch her gradually sliding brother. Artan pulled in close to Nick and stared up. At least he had the good sense to keep quiet. If the guards didn't see or hear him, he might have a chance when he reached the ground. Scream his head off and he'd be sliding to his inevitable demise.

"Artan!" Matilda said.

"Shh!"

Matilda turned on Gracie, her brow locked in a scowl and her nostrils flared.

"Don't make it harder for them when they reach the ground," Gracie said. "We ca ... Shit!" A surveillance camera hung down from the underside of the wall. Artan and Nick were on course to slide straight through its field of vision.

The rest of their friends were over to Gracie's right in the doorway leading to the set of stairs. Matilda clung to the wall on her left. A spare set of magnets were even farther to their left and closer to the surveillance camera. The magnets either Artan or Nick were going to use before they climbed onto the same set together. A wide gap separated Matilda and Gracie. The space Artan and Nick had recently vacated.

"Matilda," Gracie said.

Matilda shook her head while watching her brother through rapidly blinking eyes.

"Tilly!"

She looked up.

"I need you to trust me," Gracie said. "Can you do that?"

Matilda's attention dropped to Artan and Nick again.

"Tilly, focus."

"What?"

"I need you to trust me."

"Just do whatever it is you plan on doing."

"Fine." Gracie bridged the gap between her and Matilda. She led with her left leg, stretching her foot so her toes landed on the strip of magnets Matilda already stood on. She shook with the effort. She reached over with her left hand and grabbed the higher set of magnets.

Stretched out like a star, Gracie kicked off with her right foot and pulled herself all the way across to Matilda.

"Thank you," Matilda said.

She must have seen the camera too. Gracie kept moving. She swung her left leg around the back of Matilda and then her left hand, mirroring what Artan had done with Nick.

Gracie brought her right side across so she now stood on Matilda's left. The next set of magnets much closer, she crossed over with her left hand and foot.

As Gracie boosted away from Matilda's magnets, Matilda caught her shirt.

"What are you doing?" Gracie said.

"What are *you* doing?" Matilda gripped even tighter. "We need to follow them."

"I was coming across so I can get to that." Gracie flicked

her head in the direction of the surveillance camera. All the while, Artan and Nick slid like thawing snow from a pitched roof.

"What's that?"

"A camera. And if you don't let me go, I won't be able to move it in time to prevent it from seeing Artan and Nick."

"But we're going to follow them after, right?"

"Let me go, Matilda."

Tears shimmered in Matilda's eyes. She tugged Gracie, and Gracie tugged back. The fabric of her shirt pulled taut, and her collar dug into her throat.

"Come on," Gracie said. "If you don't let go, Nick and your brother are screwed."

Lines streaked Matilda's brow. Her eyebrows pinched in the middle. She looked down on her brother and Nick again before she finally released her grip.

Gracie stepped across to the magnets, shimmied to the edge, reached her left foot out, and knocked the camera so it looked back out over the community and away from the inside of the gates. Her cheeks puffed when she exhaled.

"So we're really not going to follow them down?" Matilda said.

A line of magnets between them and the doorway out of there. Gracie could have climbed for days until she'd been presented with another option. Now, even the twenty feet she had to travel to get to the others seemed like too much. "I just want to get off this wall, Matilda. We can work out a way to the ground. We'll find Artan and Nick that way."

"But I can't leave them." Her attention flitting between her brother and Gracie, Matilda's voice wavered. "I can't leave them."

William, Hawk, and Olga watched them from the shadowy doorway. "Argh!" Gracie said. Laying her palm on her chest, her parents' rings pressing against it, she said, "Shift over then. Give me room."

Matilda shifted away from her to the right. Closer to the next set of magnets, and closer to a sensible way out of there. But if Artan and Nick had gone to ground so easily, they could do the same. Right? Gracie stepped next to her.

"Thank y—"

Before Matilda finished, the magnets shifted beneath their feet. Gracie's stomach flipped, and her heart beat in her throat. Her voice wavered. "You're sure you want to do this?"

The bar shifted again.

Gracie reached back to the magnets she'd just stepped from, but the foot bar dropped for a third time, dragging her away from the handles.

She only needed a few inches to make it. Gracie boosted from the magnetic bar to the ones on her left. But the platform she stood on disconnected from the wall. Gracie and Matilda fell with it.

CHAPTER 37

Gracie caught the handles she'd just stepped from with her left hand. It halted her fall with a jolt that lit a fireball in her shoulder. She gritted her teeth against the burn and swung away from Matilda, who'd managed to maintain her grip on her handles.

Reaching up, Gracie grabbed next to her left hand and hung on to the magnets.

The strip they'd been standing on shot past Artan and Nick and shattered into hundreds of pieces when it hit the ground.

Gracie pressed the soles of her boots against the brushed-steel wall and walked her feet closer to her hands, her bum protruding as she climbed higher. When she'd walked high enough, she pushed against the bar, shaking as she lifted her body like she would if she'd exited a lake. Her arms locked straight, and her waist rested against the front of her forearms.

The magnetic handles provided enough of a platform for Gracie to bring her right leg up and kneel on it. A delicate balance. If she leaned out too far, she'd fall again.

With slow and steady progress, she reached up towards the higher set of bars with her left hand, her fingertips scraping the handle above her. Her throat dry, she grunted as she boosted an extra few inches and caught the handle directly above.

Gracie grabbed next to her left hand with her right and pulled herself higher. She first knelt and then stood on the magnetic bar. She caught her breath while Matilda swung like a monkey across the wide gap to the magnets Gracie had originally been on when she'd slid from the top of the gates. Closer to their exit and friends, would she finally accept that as their best option?

A single bar of handles between her and Matilda, Gracie said, "You okay?"

Matilda looked down the wall at Artan, who, for the entire time, had stared up at them while he slid to the ground.

The bump in the wall where Gracie's lower set of magnets had been seemed so obvious now. An uneven blemish on an otherwise flat surface. No wonder they'd come away like they had.

Artan pointed at the door towards the others.

Matilda pointed, confirming his instructions.

He nodded.

Her voice weak and her face buckling, she said, "Okay."

If only Artan had said that to her in the first place. But at least he'd given her permission to move on now.

Matilda made her way across the magnets towards the doorway.

Better she didn't have an audience for this. Matilda blocking her from sight, Gracie reached across to Matilda's strip of magnets, the top bar now all that remained. Stretched between the two strips of magnets, she pressed her feet against the wall again. She'd seen one set fall, what if these went too? But she had to get across. And she'd just seen it support Matilda's weight.

Gracie let go with her left hand, swung across, and grabbed next to her right. Like Matilda had done before her, she hung down from the magnetic handles, her front pressed against the cold wall. Not only did she have just one bar to cling to, but she had the widest of all the gaps to cross. But Matilda had just done it.

Shimmying to the right edge of the magnetic handles, Gracie stretched her right leg across the gap. She caught the strip of magnets by hooking over it with her right foot, her leg trembling as she clung on at full stretch. She straddled the gap, her lower half on one side, her upper half on the other.

Artan and Nick had grown smaller because of the distance between them. At least they were getting a safe ride to the ground. If Gracie slipped now, would she spread as far as the remains of the magnets just had?

"Come on, Gracie," she said to herself, "you can do it." She stretched across the gap with her right hand. Her fingertips scraped the end of the handle, but she closed her grip around thin air. Grunting with the effort, she stretched a little farther and caught the bar. She gripped with just the tips of her fingers, but as she hooked them over, she found a stronger grip and clamped on.

Far from home free, but in a much safer spot, Gracie straddled the gap between the two sets of magnets, her left hand on the one strip and her right foot and hand on the other. She released a hard sigh before bringing her left foot across and finally pulling her left hand free.

Artan, pale-faced, his brow streaked with worry lines, smiled at Gracie and gave her a quick thumbs up before he gripped on again. She'd done all she could.

With Matilda stepping free of the final set of magnets

into the doorway, Gracie followed, stepping from one set to the next. She moved sideways across the magnetic strips to the other side.

Olga took Gracie's hand at the end and pulled her in with them. She threw a tight hug around her. "Well done! I know Artan and Nick are down there, and we need to get to them, but well done. We had no right getting through that, but we did it! You two did it. Now come on." Olga led the way up the stairs, her voice echoing in the enclosed space. "Let's find a way to the ground."

The others setting off ahead of her, her body trembling with spent adrenaline, Gracie grabbed Matilda's shoulder, preventing her from following. "We'll find them."

Matilda kept her back to Gracie, but she nodded. "I hope so. And thank you for doing all you could. That was insane to try to slide down with them, but you were prepared to do that for me. I won't forget it. Thank you."

"Come on." Gracie nudged Matilda after the others. "Let's find Artan and Nick."

CHAPTER 38

"Huh!" Joni put the apple down on her small table. Not much of a table, but it had once belonged to him. As had the apple. "His apple. His table. Whatever is his, Joni takes. And he deserves it. As long as he's going without and Joni's going with."

But right now, the fruit didn't matter. He didn't matter. A bank of screens in front of her. Screens she'd taken from him. Twenty in total. Four rows of five. Each played footage from somewhere else. Most of the cameras moved. But one remained static. She kept it in the central cluster of screens. It grounded her as the only still footage in a sea of motion. But even that had moved today. "Joni saw it move. They can't get one over on Joni. She's been here too long. She has too much experience. Nothing passes her by."

Going out could mean death. Every time she left, she endangered herself. "But Joni's smart. She doesn't need to worry about being caught. She's smarter than they are. Too smart for them. And it moved. Joni saw it move. And now it's pointing somewhere else. Knocked? Maybe? A bird. It could have been a bird. They have to learn to get through the open gates so they don't get shot going over the top. Maybe it made a break for it. Get away from here. Joni would if she were a bird. But she has nowhere to go."

She could go out and investigate. She should go out and investigate. Still daylight. The cameras told her that much. To move during the day came with risks. Much better at night. But what if they hadn't seen the camera move? What if Joni got there first? What if she found something that might be valuable to them? To him? "Joni could take it. Own it like all the other things she's taken."

Her wheeled board had a full battery. Charged on their power. On his power. She stole his power like she stole everything else. His food. His water. His power. His screens. And no matter how long it took, she'd steal his sanity. "Focus, Joni!" She nodded and pressed her palms together. "Yes, focus. Back to the matter in hand. Should she go up there? Should she check it out? Joni knows where they are. She knows how to remain hidden. She can get there unnoticed. She can and she will." Joni stood up. She pulled out her device that showed her where they were.

"Joni needs her trolley. What if she finds something she can't carry? That's a good idea. Get the trolly. Just in case." The trolley clipped to the thick bar connecting the handlebars to the wheeled board.

Joni unzipped her rucksack. It had once been his rucksack. As had the contents. The button. She always needed a button. Never left without one. Certainly not when she went out there. A large knife. The one she'd held so many times. She knew its weight. Imagined it cutting his throat. She could use it to cut him from crotch to chin. Open him up like she opened his bag. But that would be too easy. Too quick. He didn't deserve quick. He deserved—

"Focus, Joni." Knife. She had a knife, should she need it. And a gun. But she moved fast. She wouldn't need either. She wouldn't be fighting out in the open. She didn't fight. She stole. She took. She depleted. She destroyed.

Joni slipped on her backpack. A leather strap hung from her board. She slipped it across her front so she could climb the ladders with it in tow. Heavy, but she managed. The steel rungs of the ladder were thick and rough with rust.

At the top of the ladder, Joni pulled on the leather strap and lifted her wheeled board, dragging it closer. She checked her handheld tracker. No one nearby. Never anyone nearby. They didn't check here. Too close to the tower. She hid right under their noses.

Despite what her scanner told her, Joni pressed the thick steel hatch above her head and lifted it by a few inches. A look all around. Three hundred and sixty degrees. The tracker had always been correct, but the second she got complacent could be the second this all ended. "Complacency leads to death."

The steel plate scraped over the concrete ground as she shoved it away. The light of a new day shone down on her. Although the greyness of this bleak place made day and night merge into one dull blur. But where else would she go? Where else was there?

Joni crawled from the hole into the shadow of the vast tower. It lay over its immediate surroundings like black ink. Like it poisoned the environment. She brought the wheeled board with her. Pulled it through the gap and dragged it up to the surface. The scanner told her the way was clear. Detaching the wheeled trailer from the handlebar shaft, she coupled them together with the leather strap. She dragged the hatch back across so it lay flush with the concrete ground.

"Whatever's moved that camera, Joni will get there first."

She stepped onto the board, one foot on either side of the handlebar shaft. "She will get there first." A twist of the throttle and Joni shot away. Her forward momentum dragged her hair out behind her as she left the long reach of the tower's shadow and set off towards her prize.

CHAPTER 39

Olga led the way, reaching the top of the stairs and the section the guards patrolled. She halted and lifted the right side of her head as she strained to listen. The wind blew hard across their exit and nearly buried the guards' voices. Nearly. She turned to Gracie directly behind her and pressed her finger to her lips. Gracie did the same to those farther back. The instruction passed from Hawk to William and then to Matilda.

Matilda chewed on her bottom lip and wrung her hands. They needed to get moving, and fast. And if that meant Olga going through the guards to reunite her with her brother, then so be it. Her hand on the hilt of her sword, she pulled it out a short way and jumped when Gracie gripped her wrist.

A slow shake of her head, Gracie let go and pressed down on the air in front of her. They needed to be calm. Patient. Starting a fight might not be the best way to deal with this.

The guards' steps drew closer. There were at least two of them unless the solo guard was talking to himself. They walked with the steps of one. Perfect timing, they moved together towards Olga and her friends. She continued to hold her sword, but she waited like Gracie had asked.

Close to the top of the stairs, Olga slowed her breathing and tightened her grip.

A distant horn sounded. Someone calling to them from the ground. The steps halted. The guards ran away across the steel platform.

Olga's cheeks bulged with her exhale. She rested a hand on Gracie's forearm before dipping her a nod. She mouthed *thank you*, and Gracie acknowledged it with a smile.

After about a minute, Olga poked her head from the doorway, the full force of the wind smashing into her face.

An open space reserved for the guards. An elevated plaza with a five-foot-tall wall running around its edge. It stretched one hundred feet wide by one hundred feet deep. Nowhere for the guards to hide, she beckoned for the others to follow her. "We're clear."

"I think we should wait on this side for a minute or two," Gracie said, her eyes tight against the fierce wind. "Just to give the guards time to get away." She leaned on the wall closest to them and stared back at where they'd come from.

Stepping next to Gracie, Olga pulled her hair from her face and blinked against the bright sun. The fog had cleared. The diseased milled about as if the gates had been closed for days. There were no escapees on the steep hill. How many had gotten away?

"It's like I'm looking back at a previous life," Gracie said.

"You are," Olga said. "I can't see us getting back there even if we tried."

"I don't want to try."

Hawk leaned on the wall on Olga's right. "I assumed they'd be able to see the two communities we robbed from up here, but I'm surprised they're so visible."

"They obviously don't see them as a threat," Gracie said.

"It's not like the people inside want to come back. And it's not like they can launch any kind of effective attack against this wall."

After about ninety seconds, Matilda said, "Have we waited long enough?" Her body half-turned towards the other side of the open platform.

Gracie nodded. "I'd say so."

They crossed as a group. A hole in the floor led to a spiral staircase. "That's our way to the ground," Olga said.

Hawk reached the wall first, rested on it, and slumped. "We fought to come here?"

Their elevated position gave them a view for miles.

"Grey," Hawk said, and shook his head. "Everything's grey."

They overlooked a maze of steel walls. Paths and roads led in every way Olga could imagine. Some of them culminated in what looked like communities. Many of them surrounded larger industrial buildings.

"It looks like a labyrinth," Olga said. "And what are all those lines about?" Many of the paths and roads had lines running across them. Painted white bars about two feet thick. A light like the ones that flashed red when the gates opened sat on the walls on each side of the path. Directly on top of the white lines, they were smaller than those above the gates. They clearly delivered a warning: don't cross the lines. But why?

"Who controls this place?" William said.

"I don't know." Olga pointed away from the wall. "But I'm guessing they live in that block over there." A massive complex about one hundred and fifty feet tall and ten times as wide. A small town on its own. About ten miles from them, yet its size and their vantage point still made it clear to see. Covered in raised solar-panelled flaps like the spines of a hostile plant, the sun reflected from their glossy surfaces.

"If anything happens …" Hawk said.

William shrugged. "Like what?"

"I dunno. But if anything happens, then we meet at that block, okay?"

"That's a long way to travel for a rendezvous."

"Show me a better landmark we can all recognise?"

Olga's vision blurred. So many walkways and paths, they all melded into one. Even the larger buildings were too numerous to mark any of them out as individual. Also, when they got to ground, how many of them would still be visible?

"Okay, fine," William said. "Now can we get moving?"

"We still need to wait." Gracie pointed down.

There were guards on the ground. They were standing around a huge vehicle. A rectangular cuboid with wheels. It stretched about fifteen feet long by eight feet wide and deep. The guards all wore gunmetal grey helmets and uniforms. Black visors hung down in front of their faces, and their chins were exposed. "What is that vehicle?" Olga said.

"I've seen things like it in the books in Dout," Gracie said.

Three wheels on each side, each one at least waist height. It too glistened with the glossy shine of solar panels. It had a window at the front for the driver.

"It looks like a car of sorts. A tank," Gracie said.

"A what?"

"An armoured vehicle. It must be how the guards get to the wall."

"How many guards do you think are in there?" Hawk said. "It has space for at least ten."

Two guards came into view. They must have been the ones they'd hidden from. The final one into the tank pulled the door shut behind him, and the tank drove off. It made a whining sound as it shot away along one of the wider paths in the block's direction.

"I must say," Hawk said, "from what I've seen so far, I'm wondering if we've made the correct choice in coming here."

"Whether or not it's the correct choice," Matilda said, walking to the top of the spiral staircase, "we're here, and we need to find Artan and Nick."

Gracie spoke with a lowered tone. "And whatever happens, I'm not going back now."

"Of course," Hawk said. "I wasn't suggesting that. I was just making an observation. This place is grim."

CHAPTER 40

Artan and Nick reached the ground just as the others vanished from sight into the doorway at the top of the gates. Matilda stared down at him, but he made another shooing motion with his hand. She needed to go with the others. Make sure she didn't get seen by the guards, who would undoubtedly return to the vehicle close by. Better she got out of the way and he did the same. He'd monitor things and come back out when it was safe.

The guards might miss his friends' magnets for now because of how high they were on the gates, but they'd see the ones he and Nick had slid to the ground on. Where his friends didn't have the leverage to remove theirs, Artan braced against the wall with the sole of his right boot and tugged hard, freeing the first set and then the second.

Nick leaned against the gates while Artan used the magnets to clean up the mess from the ones Gracie and Matilda had dropped. He transferred the heavy handles in his left hand over to his right. A dead weight, they tugged on his shoulder. He wrapped his left arm around Nick's waist to support him. "Come on, let's get out of here before whoever that vehicle belongs to returns."

A main road ran away from the gates. The front of the vehicle pointed down it. A clear statement of intent. Artan led Nick down a small road on their right. Only about fifteen feet wide, it had the main external wall two hundred feet tall on one side, and a fifty-foot wall on their left. Smaller by comparison, but still sheer and made from brushed steel, like almost everything else in the place.

A white line ran across their path. About two feet thick, someone had painted it so it ran from the top of the smaller wall, across the concrete floor, and stretched about fifty feet up the external wall. A glass dome, a smaller version of the massive red lights above the gates, sat on the internal wall, directly atop the white line. What did it mean when it lit up?

Artan paused at the line. Should they cross it? They didn't know what lay beyond, but they knew what they were leaving behind. A vehicle waiting to be filled with soldiers. He crossed the line, his skin alive with gooseflesh, as if the temperature had plummeted now he'd stepped onto the other side. He halted for a second time, waiting for something to happen. When nothing did, he set off again.

A left turn about fifty feet into the slimmer road, Artan led Nick around it before he attached the magnets to the wall. He shook the aches from his arm. "I'll be glad if I never see those things again. And there's no point in going to too much effort to hide them. They're going to find the ones higher on the gates soon enough."

Nick smiled a wonky grin. His head wobbled, as if it weighed too much for his neck. What would they have done had the gates not opened? Nick wouldn't have stood a chance scaling that overhang. No point in worrying about something that hadn't happened. They needed to rest. Wait here and watch the gates. When the guards left, they could go back and reunite with Matilda and the others. Artan peered back around the corner at the gates. The first of the guards burst from a doorway at the bottom of the wall. They ran in the truck's direction. "That's one of them out," he said to Nick as he pulled back from the corner. "Hopefull—oh!"

A group of about fifty men and women had come from around another bend. Dressed in tatty clothes, they all carried primal weapons. Clubs, bats, rocks.

A woman at the front of the group used a language Artan didn't recognise. She shouted because of the few hundred feet separating them. Maybe she used the same dialect as one of the communities, but he couldn't know for sure. He spoke from the side of his mouth. "This isn't good."

Nick stayed locked in his own private battle to remain conscious.

Artan waved and smiled. What else could he do? "Hi, we don't mean you any harm. We're just passing through."

"Oh, shit!" Nick said. "You shouldn't …" His words trailed off.

The woman at the front of the group raised her metal club and screamed. Those around her echoed her fury.

"Shit!" Artan peered back around the wall. The vehicle whined as it drove off. He slipped himself next to Nick again, wrapped his arm around his waist, and bore his weight. "Come on, let's get back to the gates."

Back around the corner, they hobbled away from the angry crowd.

The mob yelled louder and drew closer.

"Shit!" Artan said. He moved as fast as he could, but from the way Nick winced and grunted, every step dragged him through agony. "Shit."

The mob continued their charge, closing the distance between them.

The thick white line was up ahead. If he could get to that,

hopefully he'd be close enough to the gates for his friends to see he needed them.

But the mob was too close.

"Damn it!"

Artan carried Nick to the wall on their left. The large external wall. He sat him down so he leaned against it and said, "Wait there!"

Nick snorted something approximating a laugh. Like he could do anything else. The bloodstains on his grey top had spread.

Artan stood in front of Nick and faced the crowd. "Stay back!" A glance behind. His friends were nowhere to be seen.

He raised his fists. "I mean it! Stay away!"

"Save yourself," Nick said before his lucidity left him again.

An explosion of white light. Artan's ears rang from where a rock struck his temple. His world shifted. His legs weakened. He fell.

The mob screamed louder and swarmed around him. Another flash of white smashed through his vision when one of them kicked him in the face. A copper stream of blood ran down the back of his throat. Someone kicked him from the other side, and the darkness closed in.

Artan came to. They were laying into a flaccid Nick. He reached out and shouted, "N—"

Someone kicked him again.

Another flurry of blows slammed into Artan. They attacked him from all sides. Once again, his consciousness slipped. But just before he went under again, the attacks stopped.

The mob withdrew.

A lithe blonde lady in her late forties to early fifties came from the other direction. She held something towards the mob. A button of some sort. It drove them back.

She grabbed Artan around his left ankle and dragged him towards the gates.

She ran back for Nick, hissed at the mob, and waved the button at them again. She pocketed the button and grabbed Nick by the ankle, too.

His face throbbing, his world spinning, Artan stared through blurred vision at the woman running backwards, dragging the unconscious Nick. He slipped again, losing his lucidity.

CHAPTER 41

Fire raked down Artan's back. His shirt had ridden up, and the rough concrete bit into his skin. The lithe woman strode away from the mob behind like a hunter returning home with her prize. She held Artan's ankle in her right hand and Nick's in her left. The crowd followed, casting their collective shadow over him.

The scraping agony eased when the woman dropped Artan's and Nick's ankles. She turned on the crowd and hissed through clenched teeth. She waved the button at them again, lunging forwards, using the small device as a weapon. The mob yelped and whined. They withdrew.

Her blonde and greasy hair hung down, obscuring her face. She tutted, grabbed Artan and Nick, and marched off. His head too heavy for his neck when he tried to lift it, Artan passed out again.

THE PAIN in Artan's back brought him around. How much skin had he lost to the rough concrete? Everything grey. The ground. The walls. The sky. The white line … The woman dragged them across the white line. She dropped their ankles again, but instead of turning on those behind, she left.

"What the …?" Artan raised his head. His world spun again, and the woman turned into no more than a silhouette through his blurred vision. The mob continued to stalk them. Had she given up on her prize? Decided she didn't have this fight in her?

But the mob halted on the other side of the line. There were rules. They shouldn't cross it. They wouldn't cross it. But the rules didn't prohibit them from launching rocks at Artan and Nick. They crashed down around them; *clack*, they hit the ground.

One rock hit the back of Nick's legs. Another landed between his shoulder blades. All the while, Nick lay limp.

Artan tried to move, and his world spun. The grey ground and sky became one. Focus on Nick. He needed his help. *Crack!* A rock slammed into the back of Artan's head. It played his skull like a struck bell.

Reaching Nick, Artan pulled himself over him. *Crack!* Another rock hit him, and his consciousness slipped yet again.

∽

ARTAN FELL by just a few inches when the woman dragged Nick from beneath him. He reached out, but his stomach bucked, and he vomited. His body shook with the effort of keeping his face from falling into the rancid pool. He grunted with the force it took to roll away.

The enraged mob had gone.

The woman came back for Artan and dragged him by his hands. But where to? What did she want with him and Nick?

The woman pulled Artan into a trolly of some sort. Over a lip into the trough, the hard edge stung his already shredded back. She laid him next to Nick. Shoulder to shoulder.

"Wh—" His words died on his tongue. His world rocked, his balance lost.

The woman ran a leather strap across both of them, securing them in the trolley. She did the same across their legs.

Wedged in next to Nick. His arms pinned to his sides. Artan could only lift his head by a few inches. The coppery taste of his own blood coated his tongue. He moved his mouth, but the words wouldn't come. They caught in his tacky throat. He released a slow wheeze and passed out again.

~

A BUMPY RIDE strapped into the trolley. The woman stood on a board with wheels, a shaft in the centre that ran from between her feet into handlebars. She turned a hard right, the trolley lifting onto two wheels before it slammed down again with a *clack!*

Artan lifted his head. They were flying away from the gates. They had an entranceway to their right. The space where the guards had exited to get to their vehicle. Tilly ran out. She waved her hands and shouted, but the hum of the cart scooting along the rough ground made her impossible to hear.

Artan fought against his restraints, his hands pinned to his sides. He couldn't wave back.

Matilda jumped up and down on the spot before sprinting after them. Her mouth moved. She must have been shouting his name.

His reply came out as a feeble wheeze. He passed out again halfway through calling back to her. "Ma …"

CHAPTER 42

"... Tilda!"

William cupped his hands to his mouth and went to shout again, but Gracie pulled on his shoulder and shook her head. "She can't catch them. She'll realise that soon enough and come back. Shouting after her will only bring us unwanted attention." Roads led away from them in every direction. They stood on the widest of them all. The one the tank, dogs, and now the woman with Artan and Nick had vanished down. "We don't need to let people know we're here."

"I'd say they already know, wouldn't you?"

"They clearly know about Artan and Nick, but not us. And that's a hand we need to wait to play."

Like Gracie had predicted, Matilda gave up, her sprint turning into wide and slamming steps, her ponytail swishing with her jog. She slowed to a walk and finally halted. Her shoulders and arms slumped.

"What on earth is this place?" Hawk said. He scowled as he took it in. Grey everywhere. The walls, the ground, the sky. Even the guards wore grey. "This is what we risked our lives for?"

"We can't leave," William said.

"I know." Hawk nodded.

William pointed at the two-hundred-foot-tall wall. "I'm not in a rush to go back over there. And even if I were …" He let his words trail off when Matilda drew closer.

"I'm sorry," Gracie said.

Matilda panted from her run. "Do you know where they've taken them?"

The vast building in the distance. The tank had gone towards it. The dogs and the drones. Artan and Nick. The main building for miles around. "I can guess."

Her face pale, her lips tight, her brow furrowed. Matilda turned back toward the building. "Then that's where we need to go."

"Bu—"

Gracie scowled at Hawk, cutting him off.

"Okay." Hawk nodded. "Come on then." He set off toward the massive block. "Let's find Artan and Nick."

END OF BOOK TEN.

Thank you for reading *The Wall:* Book ten of Beyond These Walls.

Divided: Book eleven of Beyond These Walls is coming soon. For all my latest updates, go to www.michaelrobertson.co.uk

Have you checked out *Fury:* Book one in Tales from beyond These Walls? It's a standalone story set in the city of Fury. While it can be read independently of the main Beyond These Walls series, and features new characters, the story occurs at the same time as Between Fury and Fear: Book eight of Beyond These Walls.

If you're yet to read it, go to www.michaelrobertson.co.uk to check out *Fury:* Book one in Tales from Beyond These Walls.

Support The Author

Dear reader, as an independent author I don't have the resources of a huge publisher. If you like my work and would like to see more from me in the future, there are two things you can do to help: leaving a review, and a word-of-mouth referral.

Releasing a book takes many hours and hundreds of dollars. I love to write, and would love to continue to do so. All I ask is that you leave an Amazon review. It shows other readers that you've enjoyed the book and will encourage them to give it a try too. The review can be just one sentence, or as long as you like.

If you've enjoyed Beyond These Walls, you might also enjoy my other post-apocalyptic series. The Alpha Plague: Books 1-8 (The Complete Series) are available now at www.michaelrobertson.co.uk

ABOUT THE AUTHOR

Like most children born in the seventies, Michael grew up with Star Wars in his life, along with other great stories like Labyrinth, The Neverending Story, and as he grew older, the Alien franchise. An obsessive watcher of movies and consumer of stories, he found his mind wandering to stories of his own.

Those stories had to come out.

He hopes you enjoy reading his work as much as he does creating it.

Contact
www.michaelrobertson.co.uk
subscribers@michaelrobertson.co.uk

READER GROUP

Join my reader group for all my latest releases and special offers. Go to www.michaelrobertson.co.uk

You can unsubscribe at any time.

ALSO BY MICHAEL ROBERTSON

THE SHADOW ORDER:

The Shadow Order

The First Mission - Book Two of The Shadow Order

The Crimson War - Book Three of The Shadow Order

Eradication - Book Four of The Shadow Order

Fugitive - Book Five of The Shadow Order

Enigma - Book Six of The Shadow Order

Prophecy - Book Seven of The Shadow Order

The Faradis - Book Eight of The Shadow Order

The Complete Shadow Order Box Set - Books 1 - 8

∾

NEON HORIZON:

The Blind Spot - A Cyberpunk Thriller - Neon Horizon Book One.

Prime City - A Cyberpunk Thriller - Neon Horizon Book Two.

Bounty Hunter - A Cyberpunk Thriller - Neon Horizon Book Three.

Connection - A Cyberpunk Thriller - Neon Horizon Book Four.

Reunion - A Cyberpunk Thriller - Neon Horizon Book Five.

Neon Horizon - Books 1 - 3 Box Set - A Science Fiction Thriller.

∾

THE ALPHA PLAGUE:

The Alpha Plague: A Post-Apocalyptic Action Thriller

The Alpha Plague 2

The Alpha Plague 3

The Alpha Plague 4

The Alpha Plague 5

The Alpha Plague 6

The Alpha Plague 7

The Alpha Plague 8

The Complete Alpha Plague Box Set - Books 1 - 8

∼

BEYOND THESE WALLS:

Protectors - Book one of Beyond These Walls

National Service - Book two of Beyond These Walls

Retribution - Book three of Beyond These Walls

Collapse - Book four of Beyond These Walls

After Edin - Book five of Beyond These Walls

Three Days - Book six of Beyond These Walls

The Asylum - Book seven of Beyond These Walls

Between Fury and Fear - Book eight of Beyond These Walls

Before the Dawn - Book nine of Beyond These Walls

The Wall - Book ten of Beyond These Walls

Divided - Book eleven of Beyond These Walls

Beyond These Walls - Books 1 - 6 Box Set

Beyond These Walls - Books 7 - 9 Box Set

∼

TALES FROM BEYOND THESE WALLS:

Fury - Book one of Tales From Beyond These Walls

∼

OFF-KILTER TALES:

The Girl in the Woods - A Ghost's Story - Off-Kilter Tales Book One

Rat Run - A Post-Apocalyptic Tale - Off-Kilter Tales Book Two

∼

Masked - A Psychological Horror

∼

CRASH:

Crash - A Dark Post-Apocalyptic Tale

Crash II: Highrise Hell

Crash III: There's No Place Like Home

Crash IV: Run Free

Crash V: The Final Showdown

∼

NEW REALITY:

New Reality: Truth

New Reality 2: Justice

New Reality 3: Fear

∼

Audiobooks:

CLICK HERE TO VIEW MY FULL AUDIOBOOK LIBRARY.